Chapter 1

Flashback years ago

Sasha

"Sasha, Sasha," Uncle Benny whispered through the slit in my door. Once again, my mom left me home alone with him when she went to work. I'd attempted to tell my mom that he had been attempting to sneak in my room for the past couple months. Since he paid all the bills in the house, my cries always went unnoticed.

Trying to ignore him, I laid as still as possible, hoping he would see that I was asleep and he wouldn't have his way with me, but the monster came in the door anyway. I definitely was going to go steal a lock from the corner store after school tomorrow to prevent him from coming into my room and hope my mom didn't see it. Since she didn't come into my room anyway, I didn't think that would be an issue. The smell of vodka, must, and cigarettes filled the air in my room, and I instantly got sick to my stomach. Opening my eyes slowly, I looked directly in the devil's eyes. When Uncle Benny saw that I was woke, a creepy smile crept across his face, showing his dirt-yellow crooked teeth. Uncle Benny was a wolf in sheep's clothing, and it seemed as though the only person who noticed his foul ways was me. No matter how many signs I gave my mother or how much I begged her to let me leave when she left for work, it still went unnoticed.

"Please, Uncle Benny, I'm on my period," I lied, trying to prevent the unthinkable from happening.

"No, you're not, it's not until the twentieth," my uncle said as he started walking towards my bed while groping himself. My stomach was in knots as my mom's brother told me he knew when I had my monthly. I couldn't take this shit no more, I had to figure something out and quick because this started to send me into a deep depression. Yanking my blanket off my bed, he threw it on the floor next to my dresser. His dick was now hard and ready to commit incest. I instantly climbed to the head of my bed and clinched my knees to my chest.

"No, no, no, no, please, Uncle Benny." I cried to him hoping the cries would make something click in his head, but I knew better than that. Benny Johnson was a sick individual, and yet, the family praised him. I'd noticed every time I cried, it made him want to take my childhood even more, so eventually, after the first couple times, I'd learned to suck it up and hold my cries in until he left, but tonight was different. I cried like a baby, and all it made him do was stroke his dick faster. Grabbing me by the ankles, Uncle Benny pulled my feet straight, causing me to lay on my back. I instantly started to defend myself and started wailing my feet. If he was going to take it, he would have to fight me for it. Kicking my feet wildly, my left foot connected with his chin, and that made him irate. Uncle Benny balled up his fist and punched me so hard in my stomach I almost threw up. My medium size, fifteen-year-old frame couldn't take another hit from his three-hundred-pound body, so I gave in and let him have his way with me. That would be the very last time he would ever stick his nasty penis in my body.

I stared at the clock on the wall, and what felt like an eternity was only ten minutes.

"You know to keep this little secret between us, niece," Uncle Benny said as he pulled up his dingy shorts and walked out of my room like nothing happened.

When I knew he was out of sight, I grabbed my flip phone and called my best friend, Brittani. I told her every time he took advantage of my body, so she was aware of the almost nightly

Risking It All For A Convict

Velle B.

VELLE B.

calls I would make to her house.

"Hello," Ms. Tina, Brittani's mother, answered, sounding like I woke her up from her sleep. Trying to hold back my tears, I asked to speak with Brittani in a broken tone. The line went silent before Ms. Tina said anything back. The time was now one in the morning, so I knew they were sleep.

"Sash, baby, did he hurt you again?" Ms. Tina asked me. A knot formed in my stomach because I hadn't thought Brittani told her mom, but a part of me was glad. Not being able to hold the tears any longer, I let them fall down my face. A mixture of salty tears and snot slid down my cheeks and onto my off-white sleep shirt.

"Yes, ma'am," I said ashamed. I just hoped she wouldn't make Brittani stop talking to me because as of now, she was all I had left.

"Is he there still?" Ms. Tina asked, sounding fully awake now.

"He just went back into his room," I answered her.

"Pack a bag, and when you get out of school tomorrow, you come straight here, do you hear me, Sasha? Max has the car, or I would come pick you up now, baby. Where is Tanya?" she asked, questioning me about my mother's whereabouts.

"At work. I've told her, but she doesn't believe me, Ms. Tina. I don't know what to do anymore," I cried as my chest got heavier. I was at my lowest and didn't know who to run to anymore. I cried so hard I had to stop, or I would have made myself throw up. I guess my cries were louder than I thought because I soon saw Uncle Benny's bedroom light turn on, then his heavy footsteps came rushing through the halls until he stopped at my door. I hurriedly hid my phone under my pillow and laid still.

"Who the fuck you in here talking to?" Uncle Benny said as he stepped more into my room, looking around like he wasn't just in here.

"Nobody. Please leave me alone," I begged in an innocent

3

voice. After Benny didn't notice anything out of the ordinary, he went back into his room and slammed the door. I got out of bed and quietly closed my door.

"I heard you, Ms. Tina," I said as I grabbed my phone again. She told me to go grab a butter knife from the kitchen and stick it between the door frame and the wall to prevent him from coming back in my room, and we hung up. I did what she instructed me to do, and then I searched for my extra backpack my mom bought me and found it in my closet. Grabbing just a couple pairs of pants, shirts, socks, and underwear, I rolled them up and put them in my bag. Taking out the actual school backpack, I took out all my work and books and put them with my clothes so it wouldn't look suspicious of me having two backpacks. Grabbing my cellphone again cautiously, I dialed my mom's work phone number since I knew she wouldn't have her cell phone.

"Holiday Express," I heard my mom say through the phone in her bubbly voice.

"Mom," was all I said before I could feel her energy change.

"What I tell you about calling my job, Sasha Mae?" Tanya said, now sounding agitated.

"He did it again," I told her flat out. I knew her response wasn't going to be different than the other five times; I didn't know why I thought it would. My mom was now quiet on the other end of the receiver as I waited for something to come out of her mouth.

"I'll talk to you about it when I get home," she said like usual.

"But you never do, it's like you don't believe me, Mommy. I'm tired of it," I said as once again, tears were escaping my eyes. Hearing her exhale deeply, I just hung up. She was going to give me an excuse as to why I needed to deal with it, whether it was because we were living with him or we would be homeless without his help, so I had to deal with it, but little did she know,

I was done with this, and tomorrow she would find out.

It was now the next day and my mom had just gotten in from work, and I was leaving out for school. Like usual, after I told my mom the disgusting things her brother would do she would have breakfast made in the mornings before I left, kind of like a sorry bribe in a way, but this morning, I wasn't hungry. Benny was sitting in his recliner chair, and my mom sat on the beige loveseat watching the morning show. I stood in place by the door with my hand on my hip and my other hand holding my backpack, waiting to see if she was going to say anything to me, but nope.

"So, did you say anything?" I asked her.

"No, I didn't," was all my mom said as she puffed on her cigarette.

"So, you just gon' keep letting him violate me, Mom?" I asked her, now fuming with anger. She looked at me with her neck twisted and asked me who I thought I was talking to.

"Who violatin' you?" Benny asked like he was oblivious to the fact he was a monster and he didn't think my mom knew anything.

"You know what, never mind. Don't worry about it," I said as I opened the door and walked out, not bothering to close it. I looked back at the house that caused me pain one last time and walked to school. If everything went right, I wouldn't have to look at her face again.

The school day went by in a blur, and I couldn't wait until three-fifteen until the bell rang. Brittani and I didn't have any classes together, but we always saw each other in passing time and during lunch. We met up at the blue hall at the end of the day like every day, and we walked to her bus.

"Girl, guess who tried to talk to me in first period?" Brittani asked with the cheesy smile on her face.

"Oh Lord, who, Britt?" I asked, already knowing the answer.

"Michael!" Brittani squealed as she described her crush finally noticing her.

"Did you get his number after he wooed you with his charming smile?" I joked. Brittani was infatuated with Michael since last year, so I knew she was happy when he spoke to her.

"I did, and he invited US to a party on Friday, and I told him we will be attending, so we gotta find you a nice outfit," Brittani said excitedly. After last night, I wasn't down to be around a lot of people, but I knew if I didn't go with her, I wouldn't hear the end of it.

"You know I don't wanna go, Britt," I said as my tone got low. We were now getting on her bus, and she felt the vibe change and instantly knew why. After another horrendous act with Uncle Benny, and all the acts before, I just wasn't in the mood to go out and have a good time.

She got quiet and looked at me before continuing.

"Ok, best friend. If you don't wanna go, I fully understand," she said as she hugged me from the side. I didn't know if I was going to go or not, but just in case I didn't, she wouldn't be too mad.

Making it to her stop, we got off the bus and raced home. Brittani swore she was faster than me and always wanted to race, but she knew she wouldn't win. Even though I was feeling down, letting off steam from running always helped.

"On your marks, get set, go!" Brittani said as she sped down the street, but I was matching her speed until she started getting tired. She was a bit thicker than me, and she just started smoking weed, so I was sure that was a factor of her growing tired quick. I beat her to her front steps of their duplex and sat down to catch my breath, and Brittani was two seconds behind me.

"Man, I'ma beat you one day," she said as we both shared a

laugh. Walking into the house, we both heard her mom yelling into the phone with tears coming down her face. After a couple more minutes having the heated discussion, Ms. Tina hung up and flopped down on the couch.

"What's wrong, Mom?" Brittani asked with concern.

"This bitch ass landlord is evicting us. We gotta be out by the end of the week. I told him I was going to give him the rest of the rent on Friday." Tina cried as she got up and walked out of the living room and into her room. Brittani and I went in her room and sat on the bed in silence. I could tell this was affecting her as well. My mind instantly went to my situation at home. I didn't want to go back there, but it was seeming like I had no choice.

Hours passed before Ms. Tina came out of her room. She called us both in the living room as the pizza was being delivered that she ordered unbeknownst to us.

"Sit down, I wanna talk to the both of y'all," Ms. Tina said as she lit her cigarette and inhaled deeply. Grabbing the paper plates from the cabinet above the fridge, she made us girls plates and then sat them on the table, with our eyes glued to Ms. Tina while we waited for her to say what she wanted.

"Ok, so I'm not about to beat around the bush. We gotta be out in seven days, y'all. I don't have anywhere for us to go out here, so we will have to move to another state until I can get on my feet." Her attention was now solely on Brittani as she waited on her daughter's response. Ms. Tina had already mentally prepared herself for her daughter's ill response, but oddly, she didn't get angry.

"What state? What about Sasha? I don't wanna leave her here," Brittani questioned. I looked at Ms. Tina also, searching for the answer because I didn't want to go back there either.

"To your aunt's house in Minnesota. She said they may have apartments opening in her complex. I've talked to the landlord, so we may have to chance it, baby. As far as you Sash, I'm willing to let you come with me. You almost sixteen, so you will have to get a job like Britt, and if your mom okays it, we out." I looked at Brittani, and she returned the look.

"We'll be back," Brittani said as she grabbed my hand and pulled me out of the room. I had a feeling my mom wouldn't give not one shit that I would be leaving, as she showed her true feelings for me times before. I dialed her number from my cell phone as I sat down on Brittani's queen-size bed.

"What, Sash?" my mom answered with an attitude.

"Can I ask you a question?" I asked her, not really feeling how she was talking to me. I had already called my mom when I was at school and told her that I would be staying with Brittani and Ms. Tina, and like I figured, she didn't care not one bit.

"They have to move out by Friday. Ms. Tina said they gotta move to Minnesota." The phone grew silent for some seconds before my mom said anything.

"What you think is going to be different in some damn Minnesota?" she asked me.

"What I'm supposed to do, Mom, continue to let your brother molest me and you turn the other cheek?" I asked my mother. Even though I was going on sixteen, I was very mature for my age, and my mom knew it. I wasn't like her and that bothered her. My mom was very obnoxious and loud while I was very quiet and to myself. I heard her take a deep breath and let it out.

"Ok, Sasha. Yeah, you need to take a breath from reality. I asked him, and he said you're lying. You not 'bout to mess up where I gotta live. You know how hard it is to find somewhere to live out here?" she said to me. By this time, Ms. Tina was standing there listening to my conversation with my mom. I was speechless that she actually said this to me. Tears formed in my eyes as I looked to the only mother figure I knew. I felt sick to my stomach, and anxiety poured over me. I didn't understand how my own mother could

be so apathetic towards me. She started being like this with me when we got put out of our last apartment and had to stay with Uncle Benny. I was now trembling as I just sat and shook my head.

"Hang up, baby," Ms. Tina said to me, and I did. I didn't know what else to do but let the tears fall. Brittani was rubbing my back as I laid my head on her shoulder and Ms. Tina was standing in the doorway smoking her cigarette with pure madness in her eyes. I could tell she wanted to beat the brakes off my mother.

"Don't worry about it. Fuck her, you goin' with me."

Chapter 2

Sasha

It had been almost four years since I made the move with Brittani and moms to Minnesota, and it was the best decision I could have made. It was 2012, and I was ready for whatever change this move would bring. The scenery out here was just stunning compared to my hometown. The grass was greener than I'd ever seen, and the houses were just beautifully built. They had so many lakes that were so relaxing to just sit and look at and be in your thoughts. Overall, this was a beautiful state. I was now nineteen almost twenty and had the body of a goddess. My smooth skin was a complexion of smooth chocolate, and I stood about five-foot-six. I wore my hair in a natural curl that bounced off my full almost chocolate face. I had a double d breast size and this ass and hips filled up my size sixteen jeans nicely.

Walking into the bedroom I shared with Brittani, she was getting ready for the day. She was always slow and took her sweet precious time with getting dolled up. Tonight was the skate party at Saint North Skating rink. Tonight was going to be lit, and we were prepared for it all. Tonight would be the first time Brittani had been out in a couple months, so I tried to make today as fun for her as possible. Brittani had a fling she was fucking on and ended up pregnant by him. When she told him she was pregnant, he hit her with the 'it ain't mine' and told her he had a girl who was currently pregnant also. After he cut all communications with Britt, she went into a deep depression, causing her to miscarry the baby at twelve weeks. Brittani and I mourned her pregnancy together, as it was hard, but with me and Momma by her side, she overcame the emotions and got back to her ratchet self.

"You figured out what you were wearing yet, bitch?" I asked Britt as she sat on her unmade bed texting away on her new Samsung Galaxy one of her boos got her.

"Yep, I'ma wear that blue and black romper we bought yesterday. We matching tonight or what?" she asked as she put her phone down and got off the bed. It was about seven in the evening, and the party started at eight-thirty, but they always partied in the parking lot before going in. The parking lot was like the fashion show before the party. We had to see who was who, and who was wearing what, so we had to dress to impress. We both spent about another thirty minutes getting ready before we walked out the door.

"We'll be back, Ma!" I yelled to Momma Tina as we walked out the front door and out of the apartment complex. She had her man coming over that night, so she preferred that we went out for a couple hours. The bond that Brittani, me, and her mom had developed since she became my legal guardian was amazing. When we first moved out here, she made sure I wanted for nothing and I had everything I needed. She talked to me about the birds and the bees and even had me go talk with a therapist to help me overcome the molestation I had endured. She would try numerous times to reach out to my mother, but that was to no avail. Eventually she told me that my mom had gotten into drugs and that would hinder the relationship that I so badly wanted, even though she allowed her brother to do the unthinkable to me. As I got older, I overcame those obstacles that were thrown at me early on in life, and with the help of Tina, she groomed me into a well-kept young lady, and I would forever be thankful for that.

Walking to the city bus stop, Brittani ran into one of the young dudes that sold weed.

"You good?" Brittani asked the dude that was bending

down to tie his shoe. He looked up and saw who was talking to him and responded.

"Yep, what y'all need?"

"A dub," Brittani said as she started digging in her purse for a twenty-dollar bill. The dude gave her a dub and a free swisher to roll with. He kept telling her how sexy she looked and how he wanted to take her out. They ended up swapping numbers, and he walked off.

"See, bitch, now we got a weed plug, and all I gotta do is let him rub my booty for a free sac," Brittani said as she looked at the time on her phone then at the bus schedule, timing the bus.

"The bus come in twenty minutes. You wanna roll one?" Brittani asked me

"Hell yeah, give it here," I said holding my hand out.

It was almost eighty degrees, and everybody and their momma was outside today. There was a slight breeze, so the heat wasn't overbearing. It took me all of two minutes to pearl the blunt, and she took the lighter out her shorts and lit it. As soon as I hit the blunt, I started to cough. I wasn't new to smoking, but I wasn't a pro at it either.

"Dang girl, don't blow yo lungs out." Brittani laughed as I passed her the blunt. I was starting to feel the effect of the weed almost instantly. I felt my eyes become low and my heart started to race faster. As soon as I sat down on the bench inside the bus shelter, the bus rounded the corner. I started searching for my bus card that was already in my hand.

This is why I don't smoke weed, I said to myself as I stood behind Brittani waiting for the bus to pull up in front of us. As soon as we stepped onto the bus and paid our fare, we walked to the back and took our seats. It took fifteen minutes on the bus to get the skating rink, and it was already packed from the view we had from our seats looking out the window. It was about to be a fun night; I could already tell.

"Sasha!" Reena yelled from across the street as me and Brittani were getting off the bus.

"Heyyy, bitchh!" I yelled back as me and Brittani ran across the street to hug our home girl, Reena. She was a cool ass Latina chick from the hood that I met through Brittani when we first got up here, and we clicked instantly. As we walked up to the door, the sidewalk was packed, and we had to maneuver our way around people when I accidentally bumped into the sexiest chocolate man I'd ever seen.

"Damn, I'm sorry. I didn't mean to run into you," I said, laughing as I looked at Brittani and Reena. I could have seen where I was going if I wasn't laughing at them or if I wasn't high out of my mind.

"It's cool, beautiful. You only get a pass because you fine, or I woulda made you buy me some new shoes," the chocolate boy said as he bent down and wiped the scuff mark off that I accidently made when I stepped on his shoe. He smiled and flashed his white teeth at me, and I instantly melted.

"Damn, it's like that?" I said as I smiled back at him just as Reena was pulling me through the doors. I hoped I ran into him later on in the night, which I was sure I would because I wasn't done flirting with him yet. When we walked in the rink, there were people scattered everywhere. The concession stand had already begun to develop a long line, and there was about a seven-minute wait to get the skates.

"Bitchess ain't shit and they ain't sayin' nothing,

A hunnin mufackas can't tell me nothing.

I beez in the trap, beez, beez in the trap."

Me and my girls rapped along with Nicki Minaj as we finally got up to the counter and told Mr. Days, the ticket keeper, what size skates we needed.

Finding an empty bench in the crowded building, we sat

down and swapped our shoes for our skates. As I bent down to put my other skate on, someone rode past and bumped my head with their leg almost knocking me down.

"Damn, excu..." was all I said when I saw who it was—the sexy chocolate boy from outside that literally took my breath away, his alluring face leaving me speechless.

"You excused," he said before riding off, leaving me with the biggest and dumbest smile on my face. Brittani and Reena sat there looking at me, both with big grins on their face.

"Y'all see how this nigga just damn near knocked me off the bench?" I said laughing.

"Yeah, bitch, you smiling this hard cuz you almost just got knocked off the bench," Reena said.

"Girl, fuck you...he cute though," I replied back, looking in the direction that he rode in.

"That nigga is fine as fuck! Girl, you betta hop on that before I do cuz he was fine as hell," Brittani said, laughing as she stood up. I brushed that comment off because it was something she said on the regular when it came to a nigga that I found attractive, it was actually starting to bug me but I left the comment where it was at so we could enjoy our night. We all got up and headed to the floor to get our skate on. The night was just how we knew it was gone be. Fucking lit! Me and Brittani were skating all night till the point my feet started burning. Reena ended up leaving with one of her boos, so it ended up being just me and Britt. Like every Friday night, it was show night, where you and your group of people show off your rollin' skills in the rink. The line-up was extra long tonight, so I knew the show was going to be good. We saw The Fab Five, The Grown and Sexy, and the Street Rollers, and that was just to name some of the actually good groups. That was Brittani and I's goal for one of the show nights was to create a group of dope skaters and come up with one of the best skate routines there was, but we had to work for that, and that was the plan.

It was now near midnight, and the party was coming to an end. The DJ put on *Love Faces* by Trey Songz, and everyone partnered up with someone to have the last dance. Even Brittani found her someone to end her night with, so I skated to the tables and took my seat while she finished slow dancing. Right as I started to untie my skates, Mr. Fine and Chocolate made his way to where I was seated.

"So, can I have this last dance? I mean, you did scuff a nigga shoes, so that's the least you can do," he said as he held his hand out for mine. I stared at his extended hand for a second before hurrying to retire my skates and grant him this dance. I grabbed his hand, and he pulled me up and into the rink. We found us a designated spot in the corner, and he put his hands around my waist as I put my hands around his neck.

"I'm Anthony," he said as he licked his lips. I couldn't help but notice how wet they became and instantly made me want to kiss them.

"I'm Sasha," I said as I couldn't contain my smile. I didn't know this man from a can of paint, but he already was giving me butterflies.

"So, when I'ma get my ones? There's a pretty big scuff mark on them, with yo clumsy ass," Anthony said. He spun me around and pulled me back into his arms.

"I mean, when you accidently bumped me on the bench, I think I almost fell off and fractured my knee, so I think you gotta help pay for this medical bill. You know niggas don't got insurance," I said, blushing. Just then, a fight broke out by the emergency doors. Gladly, I had spotted Brittani just before, so it wasn't hard getting to her.

"What's your name on Facebook?" Anthony asked before running off with his boys.

"Sasha Fierce!" I yelled out to him. He gave me the thumbs up and ran off. The dudes that were fighting started throwing chairs and flipping tables, and me and Brittani were out. The last bus ran at one-fifteen, and the time was now twelve-fifty, so we had time to make our bus. It was jam packed in the doorway because everyone was trying to get out the door at the same time. The violence had gotten bad in the hood, so you didn't know if this was just a fight, or if it would become a murder scene.

"Damn, we can't never enjoy the ending of our night, niggas always gotta fuck up some shit," Brittani said as we finally made it out the door and down the sidewalk.

"Girl, this bullshit. I couldn't even finish talking to my new lil' friend," I said, lowkey mad.

"Yeah, I seen you over there dry humping that boy," Brittani said as she pulled out the half of blunt we put out before getting on the bus to come here.

"Girl, I know, right? His name Anthony!" I said excitedly. Yeah, I know I had just met him, but the way he was making my insides tingle, I knew that wouldn't be the last time I saw him. Hell, that was just the beginning of our bullshit.

Chapter 3

Present Day

Sasha

Once again, I was woken up by a loud vibration of Anthony's cell phone on the nightstand on the side of the bed. It was three in the morning, and this was becoming a nightly routine for him. Anthony woke up and grabbed his phone off the nightstand and turned the brightness down, trying not to wake me up; too late. I continued to lie still, pretending to be asleep. I was really getting fed up with these late-night calls and early morning runs that he continued to do and these random phone calls he thought I knew nothing about. Anthony turned around to make sure that I was still sleep and eased his way out the bed and headed to our bedroom door. It was already open, so he closed it ever so lightly after walking out. I waited a couple minutes before I got out of bed and tiptoed to the door so the wooden floor wouldn't creek. Twisting the knob on the door slowly, I pulled the door open, not too wide, just enough to eavesdrop on Anthony's conversation.

"Why you keep calling me at this time of night? You want Sasha to start tripping or something?" The house fell quiet for a couple seconds, assuming whoever he was on the phone with was responding to him.

"Look, I'ma come see you tomorrow, stop calling me this late. You must miss daddy, don't you?" Anthony asked the person on the phone. I didn't want to hear the rest of the conversation anymore. No point of upsetting myself over the obvious. This wasn't the first female I caught Anthony talking to in the middle

of the night, and I was sure it wouldn't be the last. I hated that I put myself in this predicament once again, but I planned to get myself out soon. I closed the door back and made my way back into the bed. Pulling the covers over me, I laid on my side and stared out the window and at the trees and the dark sky. My mind was racing with a million thoughts, and that was preventing me from going to sleep. Anthony stayed on the phone for another thirty minutes before he made his way back in bed. As soon as he got in bed, he turned my way and spooned me from behind. The audacity of this nigga to think that he was going to get some ass after being on the phone with a bitch. I winced in disgust as I felt Anthony's hand rubbing up and down my ass.

"Bae, wake up!" he said as he started kissing the back of my neck, his hands now wrapped around me, trying to fondle my breasts. I nudged him off with my leg, catching him off guard.

"I'm tired, Anthony, not tonight," was all I said. I didn't want to deal with him and his temper tantrum, I hoped he wouldn't throw.

"Now you rejecting me?" Anthony asked as he sat up on his elbow. I could feel his eyes piercing a hole in me in the dark. The only light illuminating in the room was the light from the moon outside their window.

"No, I'm not rejecting you. I just don't want none tonight," I said. I think Anthony started to notice that I hadn't been wanting to give up my goodies to him in a couple days, and that was fine with me.

As much as it should have bothered him, it didn't. He knew that shorty he was just on the phone with was going to give him some of the best head he ever would get.

"Damn, OK Sasha, I see what you on," he replied to me as he turned over and started doing something on his phone.

It didn't take a rocket scientist to know that everything wasn't the same between the two of us anymore. I was just waiting for the right time to leave his ass. Me and Anthony had been together for over four years now.\, and the end was near. We met in 2010, and it was love at first sight when we first crossed paths.

∞ ∞ ∞

It was seven A.M. on a Monday and being that I had a long night, I hit the snooze button on my phone. Turning over once again to an empty side of the bed, I wasn't surprised. After hitting that snooze button three times, I finally found the energy to get out of bed. Standing up, I stretched the kinks out of my muscles and made my way to the bathroom. I didn't know where Anthony was, and at this point, I didn't care. Staring at my reflection in the mirror, I started to not like the woman that I was becoming, and Anthony was the main reason.

"This can't be life," I said to myself as I fondled with my thick natural hair. The bathroom wasn't that big, so I took a step to my left and reached in the tub, turning the shower on semi hot. I had that nagging feeling in the back of my mind, so I just went on a limb and decided to give Anthony a call. Walking back in the room, I retrieved my phone off the bed and walked back in the bathroom. I had his name saved under my boo and hit the green button, and like usual, it rang for a couple seconds and went straight to voicemail. I didn't even waste my time calling again, so I just put my phone on the stand above the toilet and stripped out of my clothes and stepped into the steaming shower.

After what felt like a shower in heaven, I was finally getting ready for work. This day felt like it was going to drag, so I had to mentally prepare myself for this damn courthouse. I had been a security guard for over the past four years and was ready for something more. I had been job searching, but when I brought the idea to Anthony about me switching jobs, he would always tell me I was fine at what I was doing or how I should just quit and let him take care of me, but I wasn't having that. It already seemed like he was controlling my every move, so I couldn't see myself letting him dictate my money. Hearing a notification go off on my phone, I decided to check my messages and emails from last night that I neglected to check when I got up this morning. Going into my Gmail account, I noticed a job offer for a Correction Officer at the county jail that I applied and interviewed for a month back. I didn't tell anyone about applying for the CO position because I didn't need anyone judging me about working in a facility with all males, but it was my life, my decision. That email got me in a happier mood, but that changed a couple seconds later when I went through my text messages and saw that I had a message from Anthony saying that he would be in late and not to wait up for him. A knot instantly formed in my stomach because I knew that he was with whatever chick I heard him talking to on the phone the previous night. This was part of the reason why I was excited about the new job I was going to soon start because the pay was way better, and that meant I would be able to afford my own apartment and wouldn't depend on Anthony to help me with anything. I didn't know how or when I would tell Anthony.

Finally arriving at work, the security line was out the door as usual. It was time for a change, and this courthouse was making me feel like a criminal myself. I took my badge out of my purse and swiped it against the screen panel so the sheriff would let me through and walked straight to the back to the employee lounge. I put a little pep in my step because I noticed my girl Jess, who I was working with today, was breaking a sweat trying to get everyone through the security check. Pushing everything in my locker and closing the lock, I tucked my uniform shirt in as I made my way back into the main lobby.

"Hey, boo," I spoke to Jess as I took my position at the computer screen just as someone pushed their belongings on the belt to be scanned.

"Ugh...girl, it's busy like usual. It's a trial today, so we gon' be swamped," Jess said as she grabbed the hand-held metal detector off the table and scanned a male who set the alarm off as he walked through. The trial Jess was speaking on was about a cop that killed a black man within sixty seconds of pulling him over. The trial had just begun, so tension and emotions were all over the place.

"Next. Empty everything out your pockets. Remove your belt and shoes as well, please, and place everything in the bin," I told the next person in line. We had to hurry up and get everyone through security in a timely manner because if we kept them waiting too long, they would start complaining to building management.

After about an hour of non-stop traffic, Jess and I finally got a chance to sit down. It was like we always had a huge rush then everything just stopped, and no one came in for about an hour. It was like an extra break.

"So, what happened to you coming over this weekend so we could go out?" Jess asked as she straightened up the desk we were sitting behind.

"I'm sorry, boo. Me and him got into it, and I just didn't feel like dealing with anything," I said honestly. Jess knew what it was because this was ongoing with me and Anthony, and she always lent a listening ear when I needed to vent. She shook her head and stood up to assist the patron that walked in.

"You need to just leave it alone, boo," Jess told me as she sat back down. I knew I did, but something in my heart was still clinging on to him.

Another person walked through the doors, and it was a pretty chocolate lady.

"Hey, how are you? You can put everything in this basket please," I said to her as she started to do as she was told. I accidentally knocked over a bucket of papers as I was pushing her basket in our x-ray machine and bent down to pick them up as

Jess directed her through the metal detector.

"Bae you forgot your phone!" a familiar voice yelled after the chocolate lady, making her stop and turn around. I stood up and looked towards the door because I knew I wasn't tripping. The two exchanged kisses before he turned to walk out the door.

"Anthony?" I said, with my neck cocked to the side. I mean, for that to be my man of so many years, I knew he knew where I worked, or he was just bold enough and didn't give a fuck. He turned towards me, looking like a deer in some headlights. The lady turned towards me with a look of disgust, like she was his woman or something.

"Who is that?" she asked as she put her hand on her hip and pointed at me.

"Who am I?" I asked, ultimately forgetting I was at work. I walked around the counter now fuming with anger as I made my way to my man and his *mistress.*

"Who the fuck is this?" I asked now in his face, pointing to this obviously mad female.

"This the bitch you were talking to in the middle of the night, or did you think I didn't hear you on the phone?" I asked with my finger now in his face. Luckily, the lobby was empty, or so I thought, so I didn't care what was coming out of my mouth.

"Bae, please calm down," Anthony said as he tried to grab my hand. That made his side chick big mad.

"Bae? Hold up, nigga, you got me all the way fucked up. Who the fuck is this, and who the fuck was you talking to last night because I wasn't talking to you?" I stood in disbelief as this situation unfolded in front of my eyes. This man had embarrassed me for the last time. Tears started to build up just as my boss called my name.

"Sasha. My office, now, please," Gary, my supervisor said sternly as he turned around and walked back to his office, not waiting for my response. I turned and looked back at Anthony who had a look of distress on his face.

"Baby, please say something. I swear it's nothing. I just got up and gave her a ride because she had court or some shit," Anthony said, really trying to convince me that it wasn't what I thought. I didn't even respond to him. I turned around and walked towards my supervisor's office. Leaving the door open for me, I knocked lightly and pushed the door open.

"Come in, Sasha," Gary said. I walked in and sat in the chair facing him and waited until he spoke. Gary, with his glasses on his face, finally spoke.

"Look Sasha, you're a great employee, but we can't have that kind of personal situation happening in the workplace. This isn't the first occurrence, and we won't tolerate any more," Gary said with his hands crossed in front of him, resting on his desk. I was speechless. I couldn't believe I was being fired, and for the selfishness of Anthony. I presumed Gary was done talking because I didn't say anything further yet turned around and proceeded to the employee lounge and gathered my belongings. Tears swelled up in my eyes as I cleared out my locker and left the lock sitting on the bench. I walked out the door and to the lobby where Jess was standing there with a confused look on her face.

"What happened?" she asked as I walked out the door.

"I got fired. I'll call you later, girl," I said and walked out of the building.

Chapter 4

Sasha

My nerves were all over the place when I got home. As soon as my job let me go, I walked outside and proceeded to blow Anthony's phone up. I was livid at this point, and the tears couldn't stop flowing down my face. Not only was it proof that he was cheating once again, he made it a point to come to my job and rub it in my face. I didn't care how much he apologized; this was the straw that broke the camel's back. I walked to my car, and as soon as I sat in my driver's seat, I let my emotions get the best of me. I started to punch my steering wheel while I screamed to the gods. I hated that I let this man get me out of my element, and I vowed to myself never again. I called him again, and this time, he decided to answer.

"Hey, Sash. Look, baby," he said as he was going to start apologizing, but I didn't want to hear none of that.

"How could you, Anthony? After all I have been through with you, you just can't seem to stay loyal!" I cried into the phone. *"You actually brought this bitch to my job!"* I screamed.

"Baby, please calm down. I swear I didn't realize I was at your job, baby. Yes, I'm wrong for stepping out, but I swear I would never purposely bring a bitch in your face. She was just giving me some bread, and I gave her a ride because her cousin had court today. She left her phone in the car, boo," Anthony said, trying to calm my boiling blood.

"If that's all it is then why the fuck did I see you kiss her? Or did you not think I saw that?" I said as I started pointing my finger at nothing in particular. The other end of my phone grew quiet as

he began to think of his next excuse.

"Mann," he said, not knowing what else to say.

"Oh, yeah. Your bitch ass got me fired, so now what we gon' do? Can you carry the load of all the bills, huh? I fucking hate you! You never loved me, and it shows. When I get paid this Friday, I'm out your house. Fuck you!" I yelled as I hung up on him and let my tears hit my shirt. It felt like I was stuck between a rock and a hard place, and I was sick of it. I had to collect myself and get home because now people that were walking past started to stare inside my car, and I for sure didn't want to deal with anyone's comments. Finally starting my car, I quickly dialed Brittani's number. I waited a couple seconds until she finally picked up.

"Hey, boo," she answered, still sounding half asleep.

"Hey, girl. You busy? You wanna match?" I asked her.

"You OK? Why aren't you at work?" she asked, sounding confused.

"I just got fired. It's a long story, I just don't want to go home right now," I said honestly. I just needed to vent.

"Okay, girl, come through," Brittani said a little hesitant. The drive to her crib was shorter than I thought, or I just was too zoned out to notice. I normally would be driving with my music blasting, but at this moment, silence was all I needed. I was so sick and tired of this nigga doing me bogus and just not giving a fuck, and this time, I was actually done with his ass.

When I pulled up to her apartment, a wave of anxiety rushed over me. I turned the car off and rested my head on the headrest of the back of the driver's seat and took a couple of deep breaths.

"Fuck, man," I said to myself as I could feel the tears forming in my eyes again. I hated getting in these moods because my depression would start to set in, and I couldn't afford that. I inhaled then exhaled deeply and grabbed my keys out of the ignition, grabbed my purse, and my weed bag out the glove compartment and proceeded to Brittani's door.

Knock! Knock!

I knocked twice, and it seemed like she took forever to open the door. When she finally did, she was fully dressed and seemed more cheerful than usual.

"Hey, bitch. What's wrong? It looks like you have been crying," she said as soon as she opened the door. I stepped in and went directly to her recliner chair, plopping down.

"Girl, Ant showed up at the job with another bitch, kissed her and everything," I said as I shook my head and lit my blunt. Every time I thought about it, it made me sick to my stomach. I looked at Brittani, and she looked surprised and pissed at the same time, like I was the one that was cheating.

"Another bitch? At your job, oh, hell no! Please tell me you went the fuck in," Brittani said as she walked around her counter and into the kitchen, grabbing a bottle of wine off her rack. Going into her drawer, she grabbed the wine opener and opened the wine and grabbed two wine glasses out of the cabinet, bringing it to where I was sitting.

"You know I went in. I also got fired."

"Fired! This nigga got you fired? Did you talk to him yet?" she asked me curiously. Sometimes I thought she lived off the drama me and Anthony went through. It was like she would be excited to hear this nigga did some goofy shit, no matter how hard she tried to conceal it, or maybe it was because I was in my feelings, but it was always a feeling I got.

"Yeah, I talked to him on the phone, you know he was talking that sweet shit, but I think I'm done. He will not keep playing with my feelings with these raggedy ass bitches. You think I can stay with you until I get my place?" Just then, my phone rang, and it was a number I didn't recognize.

"Hello," I answered.

"My I speak with Sasha?"

"Speaking," I said into the phone, wondering who was calling me.

"Hi, I'm Stacey from Hennepin County Correctional Facility. You applied with our company a couple of weeks ago. We sent out an email offering you the position."

"I did see the email, and I planned to get back in touch with you all shortly. This is for the CO position still, right?" I asked Stacey.

"Yes, ma'am," she answered.

"I would gladly accept the job," I said with enthusiasm.

"Great! We have an orientation coming up on Wednesday, the fourth. Would you be able to attend?" she asked me. Being that I just lost my job, that would be no problem.

"Yes, I would." We spoke for another couple minutes as she went over all the proper documentation I would need to start my hiring process, and we hung up.

"Look at you, bitch, moving on up and shit. Forget that nigga and boss up on his ass," Brittani said to me smiling. I couldn't stunt, I was happy as hell to receive that call from Stacey. This was exactly what I needed to get to where I wanted to be.

"I know, right? I can't wait to start getting them nice ass checks."

"Yesss, then you can start taking me shopping," Britt said, laughing at her own joke because that's what it was, a joke.

"I might treat you to a lil' something, something." We both laughed as her phone rang.

"I'ma take this in the other room," she said as she got off the couch across from me and walked in her room. That was a first. Brittani being secretive with her phone calls now? I was gon' ask her about that. It wasn't a surprise Brittani had a new boo; it just made me curious because she was trying to keep him a secret. After a couple minutes on the phone, she finally came out with a high smile on her face.

"And who was that, slut? You keepin' yo mans a secret now?" I asked her with my neck cocked to the side.

"He a secret 'til I don't want him to be anymore," she said as she stuck her tongue out at me. She started cleaning up and lighting her scented candles, so I assumed she had a date coming.

"You getting ready for something?" I asked with a smirk on my face.

"Yep. Big daddy 'bout to drop that dick off in my stomach! I love you, boo, but we gotta cut this meeting short."

"I come to vent, and you kicking me out for some dick? You ain't no good." I shook my head and got up. I knew she didn't mean any harm, but I also felt some kind of way. I was here to vent, and she dismissed me for a nigga. I told myself I was gon' let that one slide.

"Girl, I been waiting on this D to come through. I swear we can finish this tomorrow. I love you, best friend," Brittani said. I took that as my cue and got ready to leave. I had unfinished business with my so-called man anyway.

"Ight. I'm out. You owe me a blunt."

"I know I do, sis," she said, smiling from ear to ear. I walked out the door and proceeded home, hoping Anthony wouldn't be there because I wasn't in the mood to talk to him.

When I pulled up to my townhome, I noticed Anthony's car was in fact parked, meaning he was in the house. I took a deep breath and grabbed my purse and headed to my door. When I walked in the house, he was sitting in the living room playing 2K talking shit through the headset. I guess I startled him because when the door shut, he jumped and looked back. Telling his people he was playing online with that he was logging out, Anthony took the headset off and got off the couch, walking to where I was standing.

"Don't touch me," I said as he tried to come in for a hug and kiss.

"Baby, I said I was sorry. Please don't do this, it was nothing serious," Anthony said once again trying to excuse what I witnessed today.

"You kissed a female and called her baby. There's no excuse that will make this okay. He fired me, Anthony, because of you," I said, still not believing it myself. Anthony stood there with a stupid look on his face.

"Damn. I'm sorry, Sasha. Why don't you take this as a chance to relax and figure out the boutique business you wanted to start? You know I got you in whatever, baby," Anthony said once again trying to come in for a kiss.

"I'm not about to kiss you, Ant. When I get myself together and start this new job, we're done. I can't take this anymore," I said honestly. I knew he didn't like the sound of that because his demeanor instantly changed.

"Sasha, I know I'm a fuck up, but baby, you don't have to do that. I swear I'ma be the man you need." I laughed a little and shook my head as I headed upstairs to shower. "You gon' just walk off like we weren't talking? What new job you got now, Sash?" Anthony asked me.

"What do you want me to say, Anthony? I feel like I'm repeating myself over and over again. I got offered a job as a CO at Hennepin County. Once them checks start rolling in, I can get my place," I said as I stood halfway up the stairs, hand on one hip.

"The jail? Girl, you must be out yo mind if you think you working in a fucking jail. Hell na, Sasha. I'm not going," Anthony said in a matter of fact tone. I didn't care whether he wanted me to work there or not, I was definitely not missing out on this opportunity. Plus, I actually was looking forward to getting the position because I wanted that experience.

"It's not up to you, Anthony. I've already got the job."

"If you already got the job, that means you applied for it before getting fired today." He looked at me with a grimace.

"I'm going to bed. I don't feel like talking to you," I said as I started walking back upstairs.

"Yeah, we'll finish talking in the morning cuz you trippin' if you think you working at a damn jail," he said as he sat on the living room couch. I didn't even respond and walked into our bedroom.

"Niggas will play you like a game system if you let them. Boy, fuck you," I said to myself as I undressed and got ready to take my shower for the night.

Chapter 5

Sasha

Despite Anthony telling me he didn't want me to work at the jail, I was on my way to orientation anyway. Dressed in a pair of distressed midnight blue jeans, a plain-fitted, white short-sleeved t shirt and a dark blue cardigan, with some all-white Huaraches. My naturedly curly hair was pulled back into a ponytail, so I rocked my big pony fro. I went with a bare face today, so no makeup, and I wore studded diamond earrings Anthony got for me for our two-year anniversary. Like most mornings, I woke up to an empty bed, so I didn't even bother calling him to see where he was. I grabbed my keys off the dining room table and headed for the door.

Making it to the jail, I suddenly got the bubble guts. Nerves got the best of me, it seemed. I sat in the car and stared at the gated and haunted looking building until I got enough courage and got out of the car. Orientation started at nine, and it was already eight-forty-five. Looking down at myself, I made sure I had nothing that would stop me at the security check and continued on to the door. When I first walked in, the smell of metal and must hit my nostrils. I took a look around at my surroundings and took it all in.

"Let's get it," I said to myself, trying to give myself something like a pep talk. I went to the front desk clerk and checked in with her, and she instructed me to have a seat until someone called me back. I was in the waiting room with the rest of the visitors visiting their loved ones, and the first thing that came to my mind was the melting pot. Everyone of all races, shapes, and sizes were in the same room trying to get the same result;

seeing the ones they cared for. One person that stuck out to me the most was a woman that looked like she couldn't be any more than twenty-one, twenty-two years old, holding an infant child with one hand and using a folded up paper to fan herself with the other. She looked overworked and under slept, and at that instant, I felt her pain minus having the child. My thoughts drifted back to all those times I sat in a similar waiting room when Anthony was back and forth in jail and how I used to work eight to ten hour shifts one day, get three hours of sleep at the most, and be up on time to see him every weekend. I had to work because I had to hold shit down while he was locked down.

"Sasha Reynolds," I heard my name being called out. I came out of my gaze and looked around the dingy room until I spotted a tall, lanky white man that looked like he could be in his mid-thirties. I got up and grabbed my leather folder off the chair beside me and walked toward him.

"Hi, I'm Sasha," I said extending my hand.

"Matthew, nice to meet you. You ready for this long day ahead of us?" he asked me as he led me to the security checkpoint. Matthew swiped his badge and walked through and waited for me to get screened by security. I was all too familiar with these kinds of procedures, so I took all the electronics out of my purse, removed all objects that had metal off my body and into the bucket, and lastly, took my shoes off and put them on the x-ray belt. I walked through the full body metal detector without making it go off and collected my belongings, hurrying a little so I wouldn't keep Matthew waiting. When I finished getting myself together, I followed him to a conference room that was a little ways down this narrow hallway. When I walked in the room, there were about seven other people in the room also, three females and four males. Everyone looked at me and either smiled or greeted me with a head nod. I picked my seat closest to the window and sat down, taking out my pad and pen just in case I would need to note anything.

"Welcome, everyone. Take a look around because I guarantee you that someone that's sitting in this room will not make it past tomorrow. This job can get brutal at times, and we need the best of the best on our team. People with thick skin that isn't easily intimidated by these inmates because trust me when I say they can become overbearing," Matthew said as he paced back and forth, grabbing the attention of everyone in the room. I started to doodle on my notepad because he wasn't talking about anything that I didn't know. He spoke about the ins and outs of the job, policies and procedures and the do's and don'ts of working in this kind of environment. It was soon time to start fitting for our uniforms, and that was the part that I was looking forward to. Matthew ushered all the women to one room and the men to the other as we had female officers measure our bodies for the proper fitting uniform. After what seemed like an hour of trying on clothes, we finally were about to start the tour. I was eager for this tour because I heard many stories of what went on behind these walls. Hell, I must've read numerous books on what went down after dark in jail, so I wondered how much truth there was to that.

Walking out of the long hall that was filled with nothing but offices, we got to the main door that let you on the floor with the inmates. Before we got to the double doors, we could see out the large two-way mirror that the guards were looking through to monitor everyone. Matthew continued talking, telling us who was who and who did what. He told us about what equipment was for what and how to use it.

"Okay, we're about to tour the floor. May I remind you that these men have been locked up for years or are facing years, so try not to take what they say literal, and trust me, some will say inappropriate things to you, and as of now, ignore them. I will put them in their place if need be, but you guys don't have the proper training to do anything but tune them out. Let's go," Matthew said as he made a hand gesture towards the guards that operated the doors. The door opened slowly, and I could start to hear the inmates clearly. As we all made it through the door, it was like all attention was now focused on us. In my mind, it was like we were fish in a shark tank.

"Awww, shit, fresh meat starting," one inmate called out, and that made the men start laughing. There were two floors in this part of the facility, and as of now, only the second floor was out of the cells, which was about twenty men in total. Some of them were sitting at the table playing cards, glancing at us every once in a while. Other inmates were standing along the sides talking amongst themselves.

"Matthew, I need to holla at you about some shit," one inmate said as he walked past us.

"I'll get with you, Sam," Matthew replied and kept walking. He walked us through the main floor, and we walked through another set of doors that led to another set of doors that led to the cafeteria, which was filled to capacity with inmates. The cafeteria looked like a regular lunchroom cafeteria except there were lots of windows that were barred up. There were tables lining the perimeter of the cafe and tables lined up vertically as well. As we walked through the tables, I glanced down at what was supposed to be considered dinner for the inmates but looked more like dog food. They served what I assumed to be mashed potatoes, but they were extremely watery and looked bland, undercooked chicken that was still visibly pink and looked slimy, canned veggies, and a piece of bread that looked like it would crumble to pieces as soon as it was picked up.

Matthew introduced us to the inmates that were working and serving the food. There was another guy that was unloading boxes and another mopping the floor. The guy that was mopping the floor caught my attention from the moment we entered this area, and he was the finest man I had ever seen. Standing at least about six-foot-seven and a stocky build, like 50 Cent, his chocolate skin was glistening with sweat like he had been working all day. He had a diamond earring in his ear and a du-rag on his head. I could still tell that his lining was crispy though. I had to remember that I was at work and not outside in the public, so I turned away, but I still felt him burning a hole in me with his eyes.

"Behind this closet is the first aid kits and cleaning supplies if you ever need them, but we will show you that when we actually start our training," Matthew said as he got caught off guard by some inmates arguing. He stopped talking and stared across the counter to the general area where all the inmates were sitting, which made all of us look the same direction. I saw the two inmates that were arguing stand up and stand face to face as they exchanged words in a heated argument. The taller inmate punched the shorter inmate in the face, and that's when shit hit the fan. Matthew hopped across the counter and into the crowd.

"Fuck you, prick!"

"What's up, bitch?" another inmate yelled. Other harsh statements were being thrown around as every man was for himself. Just then, a chair went flying across the room, hitting someone in the face and made blood start gushing from a gash in his head.

"Ahhh!" one of the other ladies that was in our tour group started to scream and hide behind one of the big boxes. By this time, all the armed guards started to swarm the cafe from every entrance.

"Get down," one of them said to us as they rushed through an emergency door that was on the side of us that I hadn't noticed. Their guns were drawn and pointed towards the inmates that were working. I looked behind me and saw that the fine ass man that was undressing me with his eyes was now lying face down on the ground with a shotgun pointed at his forehead.

"Don't you fucking try it, Los. Let us do our job, ma,n" the guard said to him as the inmate looked up at him with a devilish look in his eyes. Disregarding what the guard told him to do, Los tried to get up and see what was going on.

Los, I said to myself as my head made a mental note of his name for some reason. When Los tried to get up, the guard put his steel toe boots on his back and lowered him back down to the cold cemented floor.

"Fuck, Rookie, let me get to my mans!" Los yelled as he clenched his jaws together, making the veins in his neck pop out.

"You know I can't do that, Carlos," the guard said to him as he continued to look back and forth from Los to the crowd. It was evident that Los was now pissed. I think that he knew what was going on, and I believed that he knew if the tour group wasn't there at the moment, that the guard would have let him up. One thing I did know about jail life was that it was a dog eat dog world, so in my eyes, a lot of people that worked here were crooked, and I told myself I would never become one of them, so I thought. Turning his head towards my way, he looked at me dead in my eyes. It was like he was reading my mind and searching my soul for something. For a brief second, our energy connected, and it felt like butterflies were dancing in my stomach. Neither one of us made any sudden moves or exchanged any words but sat and stared at each other.

"Aagggghh!"

I heard another man let out a piercing scream which broke the stare between Los and I. I stood to my feet and looked at the chaos surrounding me. Unlike the rest of the new hires, I wasn't scared of what was happening. I looked across the room and noticed that two inmates were shanking this man with an object I couldn't see. He fell to the ground and started having a seizure just as the main door opened and in flew smoke bombs. Everyone started coughing and wiping their eyes as the smoke infiltrated their bodies.

"Get up, let's go. Hurry," a guard that I hadn't seen said to us as he and another guard circled around us, grabbing every new hire as quick as they could and took us out a side door.

"Let's go!" the man with the mask over his face yelled out to us as we were now basically running down the hall.

"I can't do this. Nope. I won't be risking my life for these crazy thugs," Sherly said, an older white woman. You could tell that she still hit the gym because her body was tight in all the right places. I didn't even bother responding to her, I just followed the rules of the man giving out the instructions.

When we finally made it back to the room we originally started in, everyone sat down in their seats and started talking about what just happened. I sat by myself, deciding not to engage in any of their conversations because unlike them, I actually wanted this job. I got up from my seat and made me a small cup of coffee and returned to my seat just as Matthew walked in the door. Beads of sweat formed, making his forehead look damp and took a seat in one of the chairs. Unbuttoning the top two buttons on his all-black, long-sleeve Hennepin County uniform shirt, he sat back and ran his hands through his hair.

"This is the life of a corrections officer. If you can't handle it, leave; if you think it will become too much for you over time, leave. I need strong people for this job, and if after this event you know in the back of your mind that this isn't for you, I personally will not hold anything against you if you decide to walk out that door now," Matthew said as he looked around at everyone in the room. Surprisingly, three people got up and started gathering their things and decided to leave. Matthew stood up and collected their orientation folders as they were leaving.

"Thank you for being honest. Anyone else?" he said as he took another glance around the room.

"Good. Well, let's talk about what just happened and what we could have done to prevent the situation, or what we could have done better to maintain it."

As we sat and discussed the topic, my mind couldn't help but go back to Mr. Chocolate that was in the hallway; Los, as the guard was calling him. His dark brown eyes and long eyelashes were just breathtaking. I knew I wouldn't be stupid enough to start any kind of relationship with an inmate at my job because I knew what the consequences would be of that, but it wasn't any harm in thinking about how fine he was. It was like I had never seen a man as beautiful as Los was. I shook my head as to shake the thought out of my mind and focused back to the orientation because this definitely wasn't that. I knew better than that.

Chapter 6

Sasha

It had now been thirty days of gruesome training that we had to do, and I was over it. I was basically getting tossed around every day as part of learning tactical training. I wasn't a small girl, but damn, my body was hurting like I just got hit by a truck. It was Friday and training ended early today, and I was happy as hell about that. I decided that I was going to take a shower before I got dressed because they worked us hard today.

"Girl, you gon' have to teach me to hit that pressure point shit. I can't get it for nothing," Angie, this ghetto white girl, said. Somehow, Angie snuck through the cracks of the hiring process because I didn't see how she even got beyond the first interview. Don't get me wrong, she was cool as hell, but I didn't think this was a job she would stick to.

"You know I got you. We may have to take one of the dudes, so my girl gotta be on point," I joked with her. We exchanged numbers a couple days into training, so she told me she'd hit me up when she got home. I grabbed my mini gym bag and walked out the room we were training in and proceeded to the elevators to head down to the locker room. As I rounded the corner, Los was standing at the elevators, cleaning the brass elevator door. If he hadn't seen me as soon as I hit the corner, I probably would have turned back around, but it was too late. There was a crowd of guards waiting to get on the elevator as well, and by the time I actually made it down the hall, the doors had shut.

Fuck! I said to myself because now I was forced to face the inmate I had an unusual eye connection with. Every time

I thought about that I laughed. My stomach was in knots as I stood next to Los. I toyed with my pen as I felt a wave of nervousness come over me, and I didn't know why. I was sure he knew it felt awkward, but I knew if I moved away from him, that would be even more weird, and the crazy part was he wasn't trying to hide the fact that he was looking at me either. It was like he knew I was trying to avoid eye contact with him, and he loved that. Los looked around the halls making sure no one else was there with us before he spoke.

"How you doin'?" he asked with the biggest and prettiest smile I'd seen a man have.

"I'm good, and you?" I asked, giving him a sly smile, knowing my dumb ass wanted to cheese from ear to ear. This man was beautiful. He had a smooth, dark-chocolate complexion and stood about six-foot-six if I could take a guess. I tried not to let him see me admiring his body, but I couldn't help it. I could tell that he worked out because his arms were well defined, and I could see veins popping through his arms. His hands were big and soft-looking, and his nails were clean which was a major turn on. It was like a mix of Lance Gross and Tyrese.

"I don't know why you keep trying not to look at me when you see me staring at you like a creep. You know you look good, don't you?" Los asked as he struck a funny pose, and I couldn't help but laugh.

"I don't think you are supposed to be talking to me, sir," I said, knowing I didn't want him to stop talking to me.

"You know I don't. What, you gon' tell on me, officer?" Los replied right as the elevator door made it to our floor.

"My name Carlos, but they call me Los," he said to me as I got on the elevator.

"I know," I replied back to him as I stepped into the elevator, biting my lip to keep from smiling.

"It's OK. You ain't gotta tell me your name. I'll figure it out!" Los yelled through the closing doors. My stomach was damn near in my ass now. This was some crazy shit. It was like he was reading my mind like a book. Yes, every time I passed by him as I was walking from one office to another, I would purposely not look at him, yet I didn't think he noticed. I guess he was noticing me. I made it to the bottom floor and walked into the locker room. Luckily, it was empty, so I picked the cleanest looking shower and tried to make it as quick as possible. It was the summertime in Minnesota, so I wasn't trying to go out in that heat after sweating for eight hours. When I finished, I gathered my things and headed out. I had to go get ready for this double date. Yes, Anthony had convinced me to let him take me out because he seemed to think I was over the fact that I caught him cheating. I was being extremely naive by even still giving him the time of day, but every woman had to go through her being stupid over a man phase before they got their reality check. Brittani and her boo were going out, so we decided to make this a double date. I was surprised that Anthony wanted to go because when I used to even mention Brittani's name, he would have a fit and go on about how I shouldn't hang with her because she was a hoe and all the extra stuff.

When I arrived home, Anthony wasn't home yet, but he sent me a text saying that he was handling business and would be back in time for our date night. I just replied okay and sat my phone down on my bed and walked to the kitchen to look for something to snack on before our dinner. I had changed out of my uniform, and I was walking around in a t-shirt and my panties. I had turned the AC on before I left for work because it was a hot day, so the house was a bit chilly. I decided to warm up my leftover food in the oven that I got from yesterday's lunch which was my famous daves I had delivered to work for my lunch break. I lit the half a blunt I had smoked last night that I put out before I went to bed and smoked while my food heated up. Deciding to take this time to look for something to wear while my food cooked, I went back to my room and straight to the closet. When I was at work, I was thinking about my outfit, so I already had an idea of what I was going to wear tonight. I pulled out my simple yet cute salmon pink two-piece skirt set and paired that with my nude and white Air Maxes. I pulled my hair into a high ponytail then wrapped it in a ninja bun. Smelling something burning, I remembered that I had had warmed up my food and forgot about it.

Dammit! I said to myself as I threw my food in the garbage. Normally I wouldn't throw food in the trash, but this time I actually burnt it up. I went back upstairs and decided to get in the shower and get dressed for the evening. It was almost seven o'clock, and I knew Anthony would be calling me telling me he was already outside, so I put a little pep in my step. It took me all of forty-five minutes to get dressed completely, and I was ready to be seen. I put on some eyeliner and mascara and dabbed some lip gloss on my full, juicy lips and called it a day. It was now seven-fifteen, and I called Anthony just as he was pulling up.

"I'm outside, boo," he said. I grabbed my wristlet off the bed and made sure I had all my proper credentials and headed out the door. When I made it to the car, I noticed he had just gone to the barbershop and copped him another outfit because I never saw the clothes that he had on.

"Damn, who you getting all spiffy for?" I said as I sat in the air conditioned 2018 Buick Lesabre. He had the inside decked out with red and black leather interior and inside smelled like the new car smell, as if he had just gotten it cleaned.

"You muthafucka. I can't look good for my baby?" he asked as he flashed his gold grill at me. Anthony knew I hated that thing in his mouth, and he only wore it when he was with me just to annoy me.

"Yeah, OK, nigga," I said as I turned my lip up. I gave myself the pep talk of staying positive tonight and not let my thoughts ruin my night.

"You lookin' good today, baby. You know how I like to see light colors on your chocolate skin," he said as he placed his hand on my thigh, rubbing up and down with his fingertips which he knew would turn me on. We got on the highway, and he handed me some weed and a swisher to roll up while we rode, and I did that just. Sparking it up, I handed it to him.

"So, how was your day, boo? Them jailbird ass niggas ain't tried to holla at you yet?" he asked while inhaling the blunt.

"You know they do, but I ain't on that shit. I want my job, and I aint gon' let shit stop that."

"Oh, so not because you got a man, but because you like your job?" he questioned as he looked from me back to the road. I had a feeling he was going to do something that would make me regret coming on this date in the first place.

"It's not like that, dude. Please don't start," I said as he handed me the blunt.

"Nah, I'm fucking with you, but I'm glad you like it. I know you were tired of that damn courthouse."

"Hell yeah, I was." I laughed. The ride didn't last that long because we weren't too far from our house. We pulled up to the Los Ocampos, a Mexican restaurant that served the best authentic Mexican food in town. We got out and walked in and saw Brittani and her date hugged up at the table.

"There they go," I said just as Brittani looked up and saw us and started waving. The waiter walked us to our seats and gave us our menu.

"Y'all, this is Nasheed, Nasheed, this is Sasha and her man, Anthony."

"What's going on?" Anthony said as the two men slapped hands, and me and Nasheed shook hands.

"What were you doing all day, bitch?" Brittani asked as she took a sip on her Remy she had ordered from the bar.

"Girl, work, and that's it."

"Oh, yeah, Mrs. Officer, Mrs. Officer," she said as she started singing Bobby Valentino. The waitress came and took our orders. I ordered a cajun surf and turf, and Anthony ordered some wings and fries.

"So, how you been, Anthony?" Brittani asked. He cleared his throat like his food went down the wrong pipe and wiped his mouth with the napkin.

"I been ight, getting money like always," he answered as he put his arm around my chair.

"Every nigga getting money, let them tell it. Nah, I'm fucking with you," she said as she laughed to herself.

"So, how long y'all been dating?" I asked, sipping my long island iced tea. I knew this was going to be my only drink because they made the drink so strong, I could smell the vodka before I took a sip.

"A couple months," Brittani answered before he had the chance to say anything. I knew she was lying because as soon as she said months, Nasheed looked at her sideways but didn't say anything.

"That's what's up," Anthony said. The night went on for a while as we all just sat and vibed, talked and laughed a bit. I could honestly admit the night was going better than I could admit.

"So, we gon' go play some pool or what? Y'all got me in the mood now," Nasheed said, referencing our talks about heading to the bar from earlier. As I was talking with Anthony about what he wanted to do, I felt a leg brush up against mine. I brushed it off the first time because I thought it might have been an accident, plus I didn't know whose foot it was, so I didn't say anything.

"Nah, I gotta go to work in the morning, so I'ma pass on that, but we gon' have to rearrange that and do another date night?" I said as I looked at Anthony.

"Yeah, we gon' have to do it, bra, you a cool dude," Anthony said.

"Of course. I'ma excuse myself and go to the bathroom before we dip out," Nasheed said as he got up from the table. I grabbed my phone and started checking my notifications because by then the night was over. I felt another brush up against my leg from across the table, and I glanced up at Brittani.

"Damn, bitch, how many times you gon' bump my leg?" I asked because I knew she felt herself doing it. There was enough room for her to stretch her legs without nudging me, and it literally felt like she was rubbing her leg against mine.

"My bad. I didn't mean to, damn, girl," she said, popping her neck to the side. I didn't say anything after that and finished scrolling on my phone. I so happened to glance up and see Brittani smirking at Anthony, and for a second, I thought I was tripping. I thought I had noticed her glancing at him and talking to him more than she usually would when Anthony was around, but once again, I decided to bite my tongue. Nasheed finally got back to the table, and the guys paid the bills, and we stood to leave and said our goodbyes.

When we got back to the car, I got in the passenger seat, and my mind got to racing. Something didn't feel right tonight, and I didn't want to think the unthinkable. I decided not to say anything because I didn't feel like staying up arguing all night. When we finally got back home, we both went straight into the bedroom and prepared for bed. I didn't feel like getting in the shower, so I stripped out of my outfit and went in the drawer and got me some shorts and a muscle shirt while Anthony stripped completely naked and sat on the bed and toyed with his phone before getting in the shower. He stood up and walked to the dresser and rolled him a blunt and grabbed his towel off the chair we had sitting in the corner and walked to the bathroom. I glanced over and noticed he left his phone sitting on the bed, and my heart started racing a mile a minute.

"Don't do it, Sasha. Don't do it to yourself." I tried to convince myself not to set myself up for failure, and I did anyway because as soon as I heard the bathroom door close and the water turn on, I lunged for the phone so fast I slipped off the edge and ended up falling off the other end of the bed. I didn't care, though; I got up and walked back over to my side of the bed like nothing happened. I entered the password he didn't think I knew, and the phone unlocked immediately. I went straight to the text messages and saw nothing but females' names. I went to the call log and started to dial Brittani's number. Anthony shouldn't have Brittani's number in his phone what so ever, so when I entered her number in Anthony's phone, the name Mario popped up as a recent call. Just then I heard the bathroom door open, and I hurried up and pressed the home button and locked the phone back and threw it back on the bed where it was originally. He walked in and grabbed his phone off the bed while I acted like I was into something on my phone, knowing deep down inside, I wanted to choke this nigga. It all made sense now. Brittani wasn't accidentally kicking my leg; she was rubbing her leg against mine thinking it was Anthony. I even caught her glancing at him a couple times, but I didn't think much of it. At this point, I was livid, and my hands couldn't stop shaking. My man and best friend? Nah, I did't think they would no shit like that, I didn't think.

Chapter 7

Carlos

"Aye nigga, how you see your life in five years?" Nas asked as he inhaled the smoke from the Backwood they rolled a couple minutes ago. Carlos looked at Nas sideways like he had two heads.

"Nigga, what the fuck is you talkin' about? You don't need anything else to smoke, pass my shit," I told my nigga Nas of thirteen years. Every time this nigga started smoking, he always wanted to get sentimental and shit, but I knew he didn't mean no harm, but for the time being, a nigga was just trying to get this money and keep it moving.

"Bro, here you go again. I don't know what I'ma be doing in five years, but whatever it is, I'ma be one rich ass nigga, and yo ole sentimental ass gon' be sittin' there right with me reeping the benefits of this dirty money." Nas laughed like something was funny, but he knew I wasn't lying. Nas and I been day one niggas since we were fourteen years old, so I knew whatever I rocked in, he rolled with until the wheels fell off.

"True, true," he responded to me while shaking his head.

I glanced out my driver's side window and saw someone walking up, looking like he needed to be serve some of this work, so I let my window down and greeted him before he was all the way to me.

"Aye, what you need, my dude?" I said to him as he went in his pocket to grab what I thought was his money.

POP! POP! POP! Shots started to fly through my window. I looked down and saw bullet holes riddling my torso with blood leaking out of me. I tried to start the car to drive myself to the hospital, *but when I cranked the engine, it wouldn't turn over. I opened the door with my weak arm and stepped out determined to find some help, but when I stepped out the car, I was on the edge of a cliff. I had to grab the car door to stop myself from falling into the deep back hole that was beneath me.*

I Instantly woke up from this horrible nightmare that I tended to have every night at the same time, before I fell off the cliff. My body was hot, and I was sweating profusely, my white shirt was soaking wet. I rubbed my hands over my chest, making sure I didn't feel any pain or bullet holes even though I knew I was dreaming, but it always felt so real. I looked under my bunk and noticed my cell mate was still sleep, so that meant I didn't wake him up tonight like I usually did. I looked out the window above the toilet and noticed that the sky was starting to turn blue, so that meant it was morning time; I just didn't know what time. I jumped off the top bunk and went to my storage bin and grabbed another shirt and threw it over my shoulder. I rinsed my sweaty shirt out and hung it across the sink to dry. I hopped back on my bunk and laid back down, resting my head on my forearms. I stared at the dark ceiling and began to think to myself like I did every morning. I laid there for another hour before they opened the cell door for the day. I already had my shower things prepared, so when the door slid open, I rushed out and to the bathroom in hopes to be one of the first ones in it so I could get in and get out.

As soon as I made it to the bathroom, I saw a known queer nigga continuously looking around the corner to the doors then behind him. I inhaled deeply because I knew what was going on already. I rounded the corner and walked in the bathroom and saw a big dude laying a towel on the nasty shower floor getting ridden on by this skinny transgender nigga with braids. In these walls, you learned to mind your damn business, no matter what it was.

"Damn, don't y'all know how to close the damn curtain?

Don't nobody wanna see that shit," I said as I snatched the curtain closed.

"Nigga, all you had to do is look the other way like everybody else that walk up in this muthafucka. Fuck," the skinny dude said as he started to moan. I couldn't stand being in jail—this shit was no joke. I went in the stall that I normally went in and closed the curtain behind me. I took the small piece of thread that one of the other inmates cut from the curtain and tied it around this screw on the wall closing the curtain all the way, giving me some privacy without the other inmates looking in my stall. I tied my soap around my wrist with the string that I had already attached when I first started using the soap, and I washed myself up in the lukewarm shower. I stood still for a moment to make sure the niggas that were fucking had walked out, and when I didn't hear anything anymore, I handled my business.

It wasn't easy being around niggas all day, so when my shower time came, I made sure to get my rocks off. One thing I could say was that my daddy blessed me to the fullest with what I was working with below the belt. I was a good nine inches, and my monsta was thicker than Megan the Stallion's fine ass. As I got my dick slippery with soap, my mind went back to the new guard that we had working here now, Sasha. Yeah, I finally learned her name through the grape vine. Every nigga in the pen had talked about breaking her off or what they would do to her if they ever got a chance. Sasha was fine as hell. Her hips were spread farther than the Mississippi River, and I bet her pussy felt just as wet. I got the chance to stand toe to toe with her, but she looked like she was an average five-foot-five at least. She had the most beautiful smile that I had ever seen, even when I wasn't behind bars. The bitches I used to fuck didn't have shit on her. It didn't take me long to get my rocks off because I knew I was on a time limit, and I didn't want nobody coming in my stall on some other shit, so I busted my nut and washed myself up and hurried out of the bathroom.

When I saw Sasha getting on the elevator that day, I couldn't help myself but to make some kind of connection with her, in hopes that she wasn't the type of female that ran to the white man if I shot my shot. When I saw that she was actually engaging in conversation with me, I knew she wouldn't be hard to break, and by that, I meant she wouldn't be hard to snag. You could always tell the stuck up guards from the ones that were going. Being that I was facing twenty years in the bitch, I had to make myself a name, and if niggas feared you in the pen, you were untouchable in their eyes, and that's how I needed it to be. After getting popped off for another nigga business, and the niggas that I considered to be my niggas not even sent a nigga a dollar, visit, or nothing, I knew I was in this shit by myself, so I needed that outside help to continue to bring in my money, and what better way than inside help?

It was now about nine-thirty in the morning, and I decided that I was going to try and win some commissary by beating these niggas asses in spades. We either played for food, cigarettes, or even shanks, but when I entered this game, my mind was on the shank. It wouldn't be long before I had my drugs smuggled in, and then I could definitely be on top, and if I couldn't woo Sasha to be my mule, then another one of these hoes would. All I had to do was make broken promises and tell them how this dick was going to rearrange their insides when I got out, and WA-LAH! I got them right where I want them.

"I got next," I said as I sat my six-foot-six-frame, two-hundred-and-ten-pound body down on the tiny milk crate that was sitting next to the table.

"Fosho," Boss said, one of the old heads that wa facing life in this hell hole. One thing Big Meech told me the last time I talked to him was to get in good with a couple old heads and a couple young bucks. The old heads would put you up on game while the youngins would do all the dirty work for you if you got in good with them, and ever since then, I had been trying to play my cards right and connect with the right people.

As I waited for my turn on the table, I looked over and saw Nick, one of the guards, looking my way.

"I'll be right back, don't let nobody take my spot, nigga," I said to Boss as I walked over to where the guard was standing. He was leaning against the wall watching everyone, so I went and sat at the table a couple feet from where Nick was standing.

"So, do we have any news yet?" I asked him without looking directly at him. Nick and I had been doing a little side business together for the last couple months, and it seemed to be going pretty smooth for now. I would have one of my shorties on the outside drop him off some cash, and in exchange, he would sneak me in some weed or that K2 shit people be smoking, and I would get that shit off in about two days in the pen, but lately, he hadn't been wanting to do it, so I had to start looking at other ways to keep my money flowing.

"Yeah, it ain't lookin' too good. They about to start this new procedure where we will have to get searched thoroughly, and I'm not going to go down for nobody, so this will be my last time, and after this you'll have to find someone new, man, sorry," Nick said as he walked off. This was what I was trying to prevent. I needed to find someone and quick because if I didn't, that meant someone else would be on the same thing I was on, and they'd find someone to bring that shit in, and I'd be knocked back off. You had to keep up your game, or it would be easy to get knocked off your square. I walked back over to the table just as the game ended and took my seat across from Boss. He was always my partner because I knew his ways and how he played, just as he knew my tactics while playing. If whoever we played against was a rookie, we definitely were cheating our way to win, and if that person didn't catch on, that would be on them. When I took my seat, the dude we were going to play against got up from the table and let someone else take the heat because he knew exactly how I was coming. Just as we were about to start the game, I was called for a visitor. I didn't think I had anyone on the list, so I was confused as to who was coming to see me today. I put my cards down on the table and walked over to another guard who I was also cool with.

"You know who it is?" I asked Mikey.

"Nah, I was just ordered to come get you and bring you down there."

We walked past the cafe and down the hall to a separate elevator that led to the visiting rooms. The moment we stepped out of the elevator, I spotted Sasha's beautiful ass. Luckily, I was with a guard that I fucked with, so he let me do my thang. I looked up and down the halls to make sure no one else was present, and when I got within ear shot, I started my flirtatious ways. She didn't see us walking up, so when I spoke, it made her jump a bit.

"I knew I would be seeing your beautiful face again," I said, flashing her my award-winning smile I knew melted her insides. I found out that my smile and deep dimples would get a female to drop them drawers, so I tended to use that to my advantage.

"Hi, inmate," she said, once again acting as if she wasn't happy to see me. Even though we hadn't really had a full-fledged conversation, you could tell when a woman was feeling you, because if she wasn't, she would have been gone to the ward about me talking to her.

"Carlos, but you can call me baby," I said, not caring how corny I sounded.

"Carlos, I will not be calling you baby, but you can call me Officer Reynolds," Sasha said, trying not to smile, but it didn't work.

"I know your name, Officer Sasha. It's my job to learn about the lady I see in my future. You'll be surprised what we can find out behind these walls, baby," I said as Officer Mikey started to pull me towards the visitation room. I smiled at her once again without saying anything and walked off. I knew deep down inside she was crushing on me, and I planned to use that to my full advantage.

When I walked in visitation, I instantly grew irritated seeing my lawyer and his colleague sitting at the table. I wasn't expecting a visitor today, so I was surprised as well. I took my seat across from my guests and let the guard take my cuffs off, and I rubbed my wrists where the cuffs were and rested my hands on the table in front of me, not saying anything and waiting for my lawyer to speak.

"Hey Carlos, how you hangin' in there?" Luther, my lawyer, asked me like I was in the hospital or something.

"Nigga, I'm in jail, how you think I'm doing?" I asked him with my lips turned up. I wanted a new lawyer, but a nigga's funds weren't looking right, and I would be damned if I owed anyone money for a job they got paid to do, so I stuck with the sucka ass lawyer I had.

"No need for the name calling, Carlos. We came in peace," he said, putting his hands in the air. Mark, Luther's colleague, started shuffling through papers, trying to get organized and kept pushing his glasses back on top of his nose due to him sweating profusely.

"Okay, buddy, we have bad news and good news, which do you want first?" Mark asked me. I looked at him like he was crazy because I felt like he was talking at me instead of talking to me, so I didn't say anything; I just looked at him while he spoke. He continued on when he noticed I wasn't responding to his dumb questions.

"Okay, so we were able to get your appeal done, and they are willing to let you go back to trial under one condition that you may not like." He stopped and looked at me, waiting for some sort of answer.

"Okay, my appeal was granted, what more would they want?" I asked Mark, but that's when Luther started to speak.

"They want you to testify against Marvin," he said. Marvin was Big Meechie, the reason why I was in the mess that I was in now.

"You want me to snitch?" I asked them. My heart instantly began to race. I was never a snitch, so for him to bring this to my attention had me even more pissed.

"I don't want you to do anything, this is all up to you. You can tell them what they want to hear or serve the full sentence," Mark said in a matter of fact tone. As of now, I didn't know what I was going to do, but he told me that I had a couple weeks until they even got a date set for me, so I had some time to figure it out.

"Alright man, I'll let you know," I said to him not in complete thought. I kind of figured this would be my only way out, but damn, I didn't think I would actually have to be a rat in front of everybody, and if I had my way, this would stay a secret as long as it could because I knew for a fact I wouldn't be doing twenty years for a nigga that wouldn't do twenty days for me.

Chapter 8

Sasha

Pulling up to work, I almost hit another car in the parking lot because I was running late because I forgot to set my alarm last night. Even though I was late, I made sure I stopped at a gas station and got me a coffee with an extra caffeine shot.

"Fuck," I said to no one in particular as the hot coffee spilled on my hand. I had to be at work at eight in the morning, and it was eight-ten on the dot when I walked in the building. I grabbed my badge that I had clipped to my pants near my hip, I slid it through the scanner, and walked through to the employee check. I let them search me and my bags before grabbing everything off the counter and almost ran towards the locker rooms.

"Hey, bitch," Angie said as she was fixing her lip gloss in the mirror.

"Hey, boo," I said as I sat everything on the table and started getting ready to hit the floor. I was excited because it would be my first day on the floor without someone breathing down my neck. I would admit that I was a bit nervous about finally walking the floor by myself, but with all the training that we had to do, I could protect myself if need be; plus, we had our pepper spray, cuffs, and batons to assist us, so I really wasn't tripping.

"What time you clock in?" I asked her just to see if I would be working with her today.

"Not too long ago. I'm with you tonight, so that means I get to go see my boo while you cover me," she said, winking at me.

"Girl, you ain't 'bout to get me fired on my official first day, I ain't 'bout to play with you," I said laughing, but I was dead serious. I knew her boyfriend was locked up in the prison, and that had nothing to do with me, so I didn't plan to let her fuck up what I had going on.

"Whatever, you ready to get out here?" she asked, tucking in her uniform shirt as I started to do the same as we walked out the door and met up with one of the other employees.

"OK, ladies, y'all remember everything we talked about, everything we trained on?" Marg, one of the senior CO's asked us as she led us on the floor and showed us the basics. After about an hour of just reiterating what we just learned, Marg went back to her station. Angie went to her designated station, and I went to mine.

The day came and went as I learned the ends and outs of just how working at a jail could be. Within the ten hours that I worked today, I witnessed someone get stabbed, someone get brutally beaten, and I caught two men fucking in the cells, which I noticed was the norm around here, as this wasn't my first time seeing two men in the act while on the job. I even had one inmate try and show me his private area while no one was looking. I didn't report it because I had common sense for now, and I actually wanted to keep my job and not be scared into quitting. All in all, I learned that this job would push me to the limits, and as long as I became that officer they knew not to fuck with, I'd be alright.

It was becoming nightfall, and we were about to lock up for the night. As the final alarm sounded off for the night, letting the inmates know that it was time to be heading back to their cells, I spotted Los on the balcony watching my every move like a hawk. I didn't know how we kept missing each other today, or he must have been in a different unit, but this was my first time seeing him, and for some reason, I became happy with my dumb self. All I could do was look at him and turn away because I for sure didn't want to make it evident that I had any kind of connection with him, so I ignored him as best as I could.

"Sasha, go check the doors upstairs," I was instructed by one of the other guards, and that's all I needed to hear. I adjusted my duty belt and walked up the two flights of stairs and took a left turn to start on the left side of the floor. I walked past each door, glancing in the cell and making sure the inmates weren't doing anything they weren't supposed to be doing. A couple males were standing there talking to one another, others were working out. I did come across one cell where the inmate had the window portion covered with what I assumed to be his sheets for his bed. I knocked on the metal door and instructed the inmate to remove the cover so I could see in, but he wasn't trying to hear none of that.

"I'm not removing anything until I get my shower y'all denying me!" he yelled from somewhere in the back of the cell.

"Robert, I'm not going to keep telling you to remove the sheet. If I have to come in and remove it, that won't be good for you. Now, I'm gon' tell you again to remove the sheet, or I will have special force come remove it for you, and you know what else happens after that," I said sternly. I wanted to let these men in here know that I wasn't to be fucked with because if it was any other guard, I was sure he wouldn't be doing this. Inmates would test you just to see how much they could get away with, and I was showing them they weren't getting away with shit when I was here. A couple seconds later, I saw Robert peek from behind the curtain and snatched it off, then spit on the window, with a smile to go with it.

"Fuck you," he said while giving me the finger, I just smiled at him and kept it moving. He better had removed that cover, that's all I knew. I proceeded to the other cells, then I got to the one I'd been waiting to check.

"Inmate, what you doin' in there?" I asked Carlos. I must

have spooked him because when he heard my voice, he jumped a little, but then flashed that million-dollar smile as he walked up to the window.

"You here to strip search me, guard?" Carlos asked as he stepped back and took off his white shirt he had on and my stomach damn near hit the floor. He didn't have a six-pack. I looked down the hall both ways and noticed I was the only one on the floor, so I decided to play along.

"Inmate, I don't want to have to come in and detain you," I said just as he dropped the pants they made them wear and spun around, showing me the definition in his back ,and that's when I looked passed him and noticed he had a cellmate, and my whole demeanor changed. He looked back and saw what I was looking at and walked to the door.

"You ain't gotta worry about shit like that. My name ring bells in this bitch, and they know to keep their mouths shut," Carlos said as he took a folded up letter and slid it through a small crack where the door would latch. I grabbed it and slipped it in my sleeve and kept it moving, I didn't want anyone to see me posted at one cell for too long, so I continued on with my round. After checking every cell on my floor for the last time on my shift, I walked back down to my post. I couldn't wait until I got home to read it.

When I finally clocked out, I ran into Angie, and she started talking a mile a minute. I stayed and talked with her for a few minutes, but I was tired and wanted to go, so I told her I'd text her when I got to the house. I felt for the letter through my pants like I'd been doing all night to make sure it was there and headed to my car. I unlocked the doors as soon as I was in range, and when I got in, I locked them quick and checked my backseats to make sure no one was hiding waiting to get me. I'd always done that when I got off work at night. I powered on my phone and scrolled through the missed notifications I had, then I called Anthony.

"Wassup, boo?" he said after finally answering after the seventh ring.

"Nothing, I'm just getting off, you at the house?" I asked him as I started the car and proceeded to pull out the parking lot.

"Nah, but I will be later," he said before the line went silent.

"Where you at, Ant?" I asked him with an attitude. Yeah, I still was feeling like fuck this nigga, and I was still going to get my own place, but while we were still living together, he would respect me, but that was a far stretch with Anthony.

"I'm outside with my niggas, bae, chill," Anthony said in the phone. I heard shuffling around on his end, and I just hung up. There was no point in crying over spilled milk, so I just decided to forget about it and go home. It was about a fifteen-minute drive home from work, and there was no traffic, so I knew I could make it home quickly until I remembered that I didn't have any swishers at the house, and I needed my blunt before bed. I took the next exit off the highway and hit a couple turns until I got to the all-night convenience store. I pulled into the store and parked. I rarely stopped at it because it was too much stuff going on up here, but it was the only twenty-four-hour store I could get to and not have to go out of my way. I put my car in park at one of the gas stalls and ran in the store and got what I needed and ran back to the car. I plugged my AUX cord back into my phone and was about to pull off when I looked across the street and saw an all too familiar car at the hotel directly across from the gas station. My tiredness quickly turned into adrenaline as I whipped my car straight next to his car; I didn't care if I couldn't park there or not. The car was parked outside of room number nine, so I got out of my car and walked to the door. The curtains weren't all the way closed, so I peeked through the slit quickly and knew I had the right room when I saw Fab, Anthony's fat ass friend. I knocked on the door and tried to stand off to the side as much as possible so he wouldn't see me through the curtains. After a couple seconds of no answer, I assumed he

was looking to see who it was, then he opened the door a little, and that's when I used my foot and pushed the door open.

"Girl, don't be doing no shit like that," Fab said holding his gun.

"Who the fuck is this?" some chick asked that was sitting with Fab. I looked at her and didn't say anything and rolled my eyes.

"Where he at?" I asked looking directly at Fab, who had a stupid look on his face.

"He ain't here," he said and crossed his arms against his chest and looked down at the floor.

"Nigga, you lyin'," I said as I looked around and saw a door that led to a room.

"After all these years, you still gotta fuck on the couch. He ain't gon' never let you have the room, huh?" I asked as I punched him on the shoulder when I walked by and went to the bedroom door. At one point in time, Fab was like my big brother, at a time when me and Anthony weren't at this place that we were in, so if I was beefing with my man, I was beefing with his main nigga too.

"Fuck you, Sasha," he said as he stood up and turned my way to watch me open the door which I found was odd.

"You want a show or something?" I asked him.

"I'm definitely about to get one," he said as he chuckled to himself. I let that one go and opened the door and what I saw made my stomach drop through my ass.

"Bitch!" I said as I lunged at Brittani, my best friend in the bed with my now officially ex nigga. I know the fuck they didn't. I was livid at the point and in a pure rage, and nothing could stop my wrath at the moment. Anthony didn't know what to do because as soon as I opened the door, he flew out the bed and against the wall looking like a deer caught in the headlights.

"Baby, I'm sorry. Please calm down," he said as he tried to get me off Brittani. I had jumped on the bed and onto Brittani serving her these hands, and she was catching every one of them. We were wrestling around the bed, and she ended up on top of me, so I used my feet to pry her off of my stomach while hitting her in the side until she fell over from me kicking her, and I got up and Anthony tried to grab me again, and that's when I focused my attention on him. I grabbed the Hennessy bottle that was on the nightstand next to the bed and threw it at his head, but he was quick and ducked and the bottle hit the wall, shattering and spilling liquor everywhere. I jumped off Brittani and ran to Anthony full force punching and slapping him until I couldn't see anymore, and he let me. I had a river flowing down my face, and I didn't care as I kept wiping my eyes with the back of my sleeves and swinging at the same time. How could the very two people that I considered my circle go and betray me like this in the worst way? I was at a loss for words, but more than anything, I was angry. I felt defeated at that very moment and stopped my erratic behavior and just stood there and looked from Anthony to Brittani. She too had been crying, and Anthony had a still shocked look on his face.

"Y'all really did that, huh? My main bitch fucking my nigga," I said as I shook my head. Neither one of them were saying anything, and when I looked at the door, Fab was standing there shaking his head, and the girl that he was fucking for the night was standing there with her hand over her mouth in shock. I grabbed my purse off the floor and started to walk out the door in a daze. I was absolutely heartbroken, but it started to make sense now. Every time I would even mention Brittani's name, Anthony would catch a whole attitude about how he didn't want me hanging with her, or how she was a hoe and she was fucking all his guys, but in reality, they were being sneaky and didn't want me around so they could do them in peace. My mind was racing as I walked to my car, got in, and pulled off. My drive home was only about seven minutes, and I made it home in about fifteen. I had to pull over twice because I couldn't see through my tears that were gushing down my face. I put my hand over my mouth and cried into my palm on the side of this busy street, and I didn't care who was looking at me. I was hurt to the core, and I was wearing my emotions on my sleeve. I dialed Anthony's number, and for some reason, he actually answered.

"Baby, where are you? Please hear me out," he begged before I even got a word out. I could hear Brittani in the back asking him if he was really trying to convince me it wasn't what it really was which made me almost throw up in my mouth, and after that, I could no longer contain my anger.

"Are you fucking serious, Anthony? After all I have done for you, this is what you do to me? My best fucking friend!" I said in between sobs.

"Tell that bitch to shut the fuck up before I turn this car around and put something hot between her fucking ears!" I yelled into the phone, she must have heard what I said because it went silent.

"Why, Ant? Please just tell me why her out of all women. I just caught you with a random bitch, but the whole time you been fucking on someone I considered my sister? I hate you, I swear I fucking hate you," I said as I rested my head on the steering wheel, and my breathing started to fasten. It felt like I was defeated in every way possible.

"Sasha, this bitch don't mean shit. I was just doing something to pass the time. I'm tripping, man, I know I fucked up. Fuck, man!" he said in the phone, while all I heard was Brittani in the background talking shit like we weren't just thick as thieves twenty-four hours ago, at least I thought. I just hung the phone up and peeled off the side of the street and rode home, fuck it.

Chapter 9

Anthony

It had been almost two weeks since Sasha caught me with Brittani, and I honestly regret even touching this girl. Sasha kicked me out of the house when she found out, and even though my name was on the lease just as well as hers, I decided it would be best to just give her some space while she cooled down. I tried to stay a night a Fab's crib, but this nigga and his baby momma argued just as much as me and Sash did, and on top of that, their cry baby ass kids were being a bug, so I decided after two days with them that staying with them would not be my move. After endless tries to room with other people for a couple days and me being cheap and not wanting to spend any money on a hotel, I did the dumbest shit possible and went to Brittani's house, and after a couple of minutes, I instantly regretted that move.

"Babe, I'm so happy you decided to stay here for a couple days, I think this is what we need to get closer and establish that bond that I've been talking about," Brittani said as she snuggled up against my bare chest. When we were sneaking around, it was all fun and games to me, but the fact that she was thinking future wise with me had my stomach turning. Brittani would never be more than a fuck to me, and as soon as my paper was where I needed it to be, I was out her crib. I'd been trying to call Sasha for the past couple days, but she was avoiding me at all costs.

"Yeah, me too," I said dryly as I didn't want to feed into her feelings much more than I already had. She must have caught my drift because she sat straight up and looked down at me.

"What's wrong, baby? You been actin' real strange these past couple days," she said, rubbing my dick through my boxers.

"Nah, I'm good, shorty," I said as I grabbed the remote control from off the nightstand and turned the music up. I really wasn't trying to hear nothing she was saying, and at this point, I didn't care how she was feeling, and if she was going to kick me out, she needed to go ahead and do that. It'd give me a reason to leave her alone for good.

"Okay, Anthony, what's the problem? You said if we ever got the chance to be together in peace, we would, and now that we actually got the chance, you acting all stank and shit, like what the fuck?" Brittani said as she nudged me a little on the side. I could tell that she was serious, so I decided not to hurt her feelings too bad at the moment.

"Look, boo, I know what I said, but you gotta see shit from my point of view," I said, getting slightly agitated.

"And what's your point of view, AT?" she said pouting, calling me by my street name.

"Brittani, me and Sasha been together for four years, almost five. I don't know how easy you thought it would be to get over someone so quick, but it ain't all that easy, ma. I'm trying to give you what you want out of me, but damn, you can't be talking all this simp shit and expecting me to have the reaction you want," I said, and that was being real. I wanted her to know that I still loved Sasha, even with me doing her dirty.

"So, what you're saying is you laid up with me but still in love with this bitch?" Brittani asked, pointing to no one in particular. I looked at her with a disturbed expression on my face. It was about three in the morning, and I just got in and didn't want to hear all this extra shit.

"Bitch? You mean the woman that was your best friend for... I don't know how long, the bitch whose man you wanted and still want until this day?" I asked her. I could tell that pissed her off, but I didn't care. She was talking about Sasha as if her shit didn't stink.

"So, that's what we gon' be on now?" she asked me as she got off the bed and started cleaning off the dresser. I didn't know what it was about black women, but whenever you struck a nerve, they started cleaning shit that didn't need to be cleaned. I decided I was going to leave for a minute. I could tell that this was a bad move, and I didn't feel like dealing with any of those emotions at the moment, especially from someone who wasn't even my bitch. I got up and started gathering my little overnight bag before she started with me again.

"So, you really gon' leave? Look, I'm sorry, Ant, I just be getting in my feelings about you sometimes, and I know the circumstances is fucked up right now, but you know how I felt and still feel about you," Brittani said as she started walking towards me. She grabbed my bag out of my hand and threw it back on the chair where it originally was. I rubbed my waves in irritation and sat back on the bed. Following behind me, when I sat down, Brittani kneeled in front of me and started kissing on my neck.

"I don't want to upset you, boo. I'll leave it alone," she whispered in my ear as she rubbed my dick through my basketball shorts.

"I don't know why you be trippin', you know what it is, lil' baby," I said as she ushered me to sit up while she pulled my shorts down.

"I sure do," Brittani said just as she grabbed the base of my dick which was now hard as a rock, with her right hand as she slid it inside her warm mouth and massaged my balls with her left. That's one thing I could say about Britt, her sex game was the shit! I lowered myself down on the bed and enjoyed the best head I had ever had.

We had finally woken up after our sex crazed session, I looked at my phone and saw that it was eight-thirty in the morning. I had a meeting at noon with one of my hopefully soon to be connects, Juno, this Italian dude from Philly, so I called Fab to make sure he was up and ready to get to this money.

"What's going on, bro?" he answered, sounding like he was still asleep.

"Wake that ass up, boy! We got business to handle," I said as I got up and walked to the bathroom to get ready for a shower.

"I'm already up, my nigga. I stay up and ready," Fab responded.

"Be ready by eleven, we got something to politic about before-hand."

"Bet." That ended our conversation, and I put my phone on the bathroom counter and stripped down to my ass. I didn't feel like being around Brittani's clingy ass all day, so I had to think of some plans to get into until later on tonight.

After my twenty-minute shower, I walked back to the room, and Brittani was talking on the phone to her sister about how good my dick was last night, and I just shook my head. I grabbed my clothes out the bag I bought out the mall yesterday and started snatching the tags off of them. Just some plain denim blue jean shorts, a black v-neck shirt, with some black Forces. I grabbed my gold chain off Brittani's dresser and sprayed some of the Gucci Guilty Intense cologne she bought me a couple weeks ago and grabbed my keys off the nightstand.

"Alright, I'm out. I'll hit you up later," I said as I started walking towards the door.

"Damn, no hug or kiss, daddy?" she asked with a slight attitude.

"I'm in a rush. I'll hit you up in a couple hours," I said

as I walked straight to the front door and walked out. I didn't know what the fuck I was thinking about fucking with her, but in order for her not to go terrorizing Sasha, I just dealt with the shit until I could figure out what me and Sash were going to do. Until then, I was cooling until I figured out my next move.

I hopped in the car and drove to Fab's spot which was on the East side. It was a nice and sunny day outside, and even though it was still early, it seemed like everybody was outside handling business. It took me all of ten minutes to get to his crib, and when I got to the door, I just walked in. This nigga thought he was the Godfather or someone because he stayed with his crib unlocked.

"Ayo!" I yelled through the house to let him know I was there.

"I'm in the shower, cuz, roll up!" he yelled back down. I sat on the living room couch and grabbed his stash from under the table and started rolling a couple dubies. The T.V was turned to CNN, so I turned the volume up and tuned in while I lit my blunt I brought in and rolled the ones for my manz. His baby mom and kids were gone, so the house was peaceful.

"This a fucked up ass president," I said to myself as I listened to the orange man talk about the wall. After rolling three Backwoods, I grabbed my phone out of my pocket and went to my photo gallery and scrolled through me and Sasha's pictures. Yeah, I know I fucked up, but a nigga was really missing her. My heart wanted to call her so bad, but my fingers wouldn't dial the number, so I went to my text messages and decided to try it that way.

Thinking about you. I'm sorry, baby.
I fucked up, and I regret it. Talk to me when you ready. Love you.

I deleted the message as soon as I sent it and put the phone back in my wallet when I heard fat ass coming down the stairs. Fab considered himself a B.O.N, (big ole nigga), and I often teased him about his weight, but he knew it was all love. Hell, he still pulled hoes on his bad days. I stressed to my crew enough that you didn't want to be flashy, but you wanted to make an impression. Always keep yourself looking and feeling good, and your day would go in a positive direction.

He sat down in his recliner chair and put the footrest up. Fab grabbed his Xbox controllers and threw me one and turned the game on.

"What we playin'?" I asked, taking off my shirt and laying it across the armrest of the couch.

"COD."

"COD," I said as I sat back and got in tune with the game. We played for about an hour before we headed up north to meet with Juno.

"Alright, this meeting is what's going to put us on the map, my nigga, so we gon' go in here, talk this money shit, and hope he plug us. If not, I'll chop it up with his ass; either way, we leaving out this muthfucka with some work."

"Let's go. The earlier we can get in this bitch, the faster we get out. I already got customers lined up waiting on that new shit," Fab said. We decided not to play the game, but to get to the meeting early. We smoked a blunt and talked about Brittani's crazy self before finally leaving out.

When we got to the destination per my GPS, we arrived at a gate surrounding a beautiful home. I called Juno and informed him that we were at the gate, and he told me the code to enter. We drove down the long driveway and pulled up to his front steps.

"Damn, this nigga living like this?" Fab said just as amazed as me. I had to admit that I knew this nigga was the plug, but I didn't know he had it like this. I was surprised my damn self. We got out the car and walked up to the door just as a beautiful Hispanic lady answered.

"Welcome, come in," she said with a very deep Latino sounding accent, stepping aside and letting us into their gorgeous interior. I must admit, Fab and I were blown away by how beautiful his home was. The thick Hispanic woman led us down the hall to a patio door and outside where Juno was sitting with a heavy-set man that I assumed to be his protector. He stood up as he saw us walking across the grass and gestured for a hug. Fab and I both gave him a friendly hug and took our seats at the glass table while miss lady poured all of us a glass of cognac.

"I got a meeting in a few, so we must make this quick," Juno said as he leaned back in his seat and sipped his drink.

"So, I can price them at twelve g's for you, and if I see you moving them things and bringing in the bread, I'll lower the price for you. If I see you can slang 'em, I'll start giving you deals. Everybody eating good over here, baby," Juno said as he clipped the end of three Cuban cigars and laid them on the table. I looked at Fab who was rubbing his hands together, nodding his head. I sat and rubbed my goatee for a minute, acting like I was thinking if I was going to work with him or not, when in actuality, I told myself if he offered anything under twelve I would accept.

"Do we need to go over pricing and measurements?" Juno asked as he looked from me back to Fab. I kind of felt like that was a low blow or something, but I wasn't surprised because everyone thought blacks weren't educated, but when you start ed showing them differently, they acted surprised.

"Nah, we got this," I said, staring him directly in his eyes. He made a hand gesture to his boy that was sitting with us, and he reached under the table and grabbed a small black duffel bag and tossed it at Fab's feet.

"I'm not rushing it, but have my money back in a timely fashion. First impression is everything," Juno said. I stood up followed by Fab, deciding to end this meeting because the shade was being thrown too far. I was starting to feel like he was looking at me like less than a man because of my skin color; I knew he wouldn't ask these questions if my skin matched his.

"You'll have it," we said as we got up and escorted ourselves back into the house and out the front door. I couldn't wait to get this paper right so I wouldn't have to cop from nobody else because I'd be the plug.

After the meeting, I decided to drop Fab off at home and make an important run, and that was trying to catch Sasha before she went to work. I tried to text her every day, and she just didn't reply at all, so I was going to do the next best thing, and that was talking to her face to face. I hadn't seen her since the day she kicked me out which was a couple weeks ago. I just needed to know where her head was at and what the end outcome would be. Yeah, I knew it didn't look good staying with Brittani, but it was what was easier for me at the moment. It was about one-thirty, and I knew she left around two, so I planned to sit outside and wait until she came out the house to talk.

I made it to her house in fifteen minutes and pulled up on the side by her car. I pulled my hood over my head and sat my seat back a little. I was tired and needed a nap, but I had to handle this first. I rolled me a blunt and turned my radio on and listened to the music while I waited, and just like I thought, Sasha was walking out the house at two-oh-five. She didn't see me hop out of the car, but when she turned around, she jumped a bit because I startled her. She took one look at me and shook her head and rushed around to her driver's side.

"Sash, please, baby, just talk to me," I said as I walked around to her driver's side door and stood there in her face pleading with my eyes.

"Anthony, you got some nerve. What do you think you can say to me that would make me forgive you for fucking my best friend, huh?" she asked me with tears starting to swell up in her eyes, and that was the last thing I came here for was to make her cry.

"I don't know, baby--I just want you to say something to me. I know I fucked up, I know I'm a fuck up, but I dont want to lose you. I swear I will do right; I've learned my lesson, baby. I just don't want to lose you," I said, damn near in tears myself. My heart was racing fast as I waited for her to say something. I glanced at her appearance, and she was the most beautiful woman I had ever seen. She looked stunning in her corrections uniform.

"How long have you been talking to her, Ant?" she asked me, looking everywhere on the street but at me. I tried to avoid the question by changing the subject by telling her how beautiful she looked, but she wasn't going.

"It just happened all of a sudden. It was a spur of the moment deal, boo, I swear. I wasn't on nothing with her; she wanted to suck my dick, and I let her like a dummy. She has always been thirsty for me, babe; that's why I never want her around because she be on some other shit," I said, lying through my teeth when in reality, we'd been talking for months.

"You a fucking lie, nigga, cuz that night we got back from the double date, I looked through the phone and saw you had that bitch's number saved under Mario. Now what you gon' say?" Sasha asked, catching me off guard because I didn't know she knew that. I couldn't come up with the lie fast enough, and I stood there stuck. She shook her head and got in the driver's seat of her car and pulled off, leaving me in the dust, literally.

Chapter 10

Carlos

I didn't get an ounce of sleep last night because my nerves got the best of me. I had been serving a total of two years in jail, and my appeal was finally granted, and I got my day in court again. My palms had been sweating all morning, and I was just ready to get this shit over. I couldn't believe I was actually about to rat out one of my niggas, but I couldn't see myself serving eighteen more years in this shit hole, especially with no support or help. The only thing that made me okay with what I was about to do was the fact that the same nigga I was facing twenty years for hadn't even given a nigga a dime, not even a visit. I tried calling this nigga numerous times, and eventually he blocked the jail number from calling back. I was in this bitch alone but had a pack full of niggas when I was in the streets.

"Nigga, you been tossing and turning all night, stop fucking moving so much," my celly said to me from the bottom bunk. I didn't even respond back to him because my mind was elsewhere at the moment. It literally felt like my stomach was in knots, and I felt like I could throw up all the food I consumed within the last couple days. I needed to do something that would keep me calm, so I hopped off my bunk, landing on both my feet, and started working out. I got in a push up position and started my push ups.

"One, two, three, four, five…"

I counted out loud until I reached fifty, which took me a minute and a half. I then started to do some sit ups, followed by more push ups. I alternated between those two workouts as my mind drifted back to the night I got arrested, which I did all too often.

∞∞∞

Flashback

Me and my nigga, Nas, were posted outside of Meechie's crib smoking and chillin' on that late night. It was a Sunday night, and that's when all the low-key fiends came out to play. By that, I meant all the teachers, lawyers, doctors; all those people with careers came out because they would rather not be seen during the day, so they come at night.

"Aye, when Nolan get here, send that nigga in the crib, I know his geek ass comin' tonight," Big Meechie said as he popped his head out the screen door. We were in the part of town that the police often times neglected, so our money rarely stopped over here. They would rather us kill ourselves with the poison we put on the streets than them do the dirty work for us, so they sad fuck it, we could police ourselves. Nolan was this African construction worker that often came up short with Meechie's money when he came for some work, and I guess Meechie was about to make him pay up tonight. We didn't ask no questions but agreed and kept on with our night and just like he said, not even an hour later, Nolan came strolling down the street in his dirty work uniform and stopped at the gate which was infrequent.

"Aye, nigga, what the fuck you standin' by the gate for? Meechie wanna see you goofy," I said as Nolan continued to sit there, resting his arm on the metal gate. He slowly opened the gate and took a couple steps in and turned back around to lock the gate.

"Go tell Meechie that nigga here," I told Nas. Nas had a confused look on his face just as I did.

"Bi-Big Meechie in there?" Nolan finally answered, looking like he just saw a ghost.

"Nigga, didn't I say he wanted to see you, so why wouldn't he be in the house?" I was now standing at the top of the stairs. He put his hands in his pockets and continued to take baby steps towards the porch, and that's when I got a bad feeling in the pit of my stomach.

"Nolan, dude, what the fuck is wrong with you? Take that dope head shit somewhere else," I said, shooting him off. He was shifting back and forth like he was going through some shit. I then saw an armored truck hit the corner and police dressed in riot gear pop out from each angle of the house basically.

"Freeze! Don't move, or I will shoot!" one of the officers yelled as I attempted to run back in the house.

FUCK! I said to myself. I wanted to beat the shit out of Nolan's goofy ass. He was playing decoy for these sucka ass cops that's why he was acting like that. I laid on the ground on my stomach and put my hands and feet out where they could see them. Other cops ran up in the house and searched it. I was waiting on them to bring out Big Meechie and Nas, but when the cop came back out and said the house was clear, I damn near shitted myself. How the fuck these niggas get out the house that quick when the back doors were bolted, and it took the boys, which we call police in my neighborhood, all of thirty seconds from the time they announced themselves to actually getting in the house?

"Where your boys at, Carlos, or did you not think we knew who you were?" one of the pale face pigs asked me. I was now livid at this point, and I didn't care what this cracker ass cop was talking about. I couldn't believe these niggas upped on me. One cop walked out the front door with two duffel bags in both hands, and another cop walked out holding the bags of money I just brought in to Meechie and other bags with money Big Meechie collected from earlier.

"You see them bags, all that shit got your name on it. Get up, punk," the officer said as he blew his stanky ass cigarette breath in *my face and pulled me up so hard it felt like he dislocated my shoulder. Throwing me against the porch door, the officer that originally put the cuffs on me forced and kicked my feet open so wide I damn near did the splits.*

"What you got on you that's gon' poke, stick, or stab me?" he asked, vigorously searching through my pockets. The first thing he grabbed was the bag of weed that I was smoking out of all day and threw it on the chair Nas was sitting in.

"Man, I ain't got shit but that small ass bag of weed, homie," I said as I turned and looked at the pig sideways. He then ripped me away from the screen door and pulled me towards his car. One of his fellow boys in blue had already opened the door for me. We got to the door, and he pushed my head down and into the car. He opened the driver's door and turned the AC on and closed his door and opened mine again.

"You better hope your boys turn up and soon, or you won't be seeing the light of day for a very long time," he said to me and closed the door.

∞∞∞

My life after that night had been a living hell. They took me down to the station and questioned me for what seemed like days, but it was only hours. After finding out that Nas and Meechie snuck out the backdoor and left me on the porch to basically take the fall, I knew I couldn't trust anyone. I sat across from the detectives and all they wanted me to do was give them the names of the people that were in the house at the time of the bust because they had word that we were all in there. I knew right off the back they heard it from Nolan's bitch ass because he was bugging the whole day, and judging by the way that he was acting when he came back the last time that night gave it away. There was a little birdie flying around town saying that the feds were trying to get dirt on Meechie and his team, so I wasn't surprised that he knew who I was and what I was about. They also knew I knew Big Meechie; they showed me pictures of us trapping together and everything, so I knew what was up. All they needed from me was to say Big Meechie was the one supplying me the drugs that I was selling, and they would have let me go, but I knew just like they knew that was bullshit. So, in exchange for my silence, they threw twenty years at my ass. When I found out that I was being charged with distribution of narcotics, money laundering, and a murder charge, I damn near shitted my pants! I knew them was my niggas though, and they were going to hold me down through this bid if I caught this charge for Big Meechie, but here I was, two years in this bid, and I ain't heard from nobody except my momma and my cousin, Bud. I even called the nigga, Meechie, so many times that his ass either changed his number or blocked the jail from calling-- bullshit, right?

After numerous meetings with my legal team that my people put the money up for, they decided it would be best if I just gave up the names the cops wanted to hear. I wasn't feeling that in any kind of shape, but as I sat in my cell on numerous occasions and had multiple self talks, I knew I would be stupid to do a bid for a muthafucka who couldn't even put twenty bucks on my books, when I knew that nigga was damn near rich, because I helped the nigga get there. Eventually, the feds caught up with Meechie and locked him up, and of course, that's when I had to reappear in court. That was one of the most embarrassing days of my life. When I took the stand, it was like Big Meechie was staring a hole in my head, and I did everything to avoid his eye contact, but I said fuck it. I had to own up and face what I was about to do, so when they asked me to identify the man that was supplying me the drugs to sell, I pointed and looked directly at Meechie. He had a somber look on his face and shook his head from side to side as I just labeled myself as a rat.

Fast forward to present day, after my day in court they told me that I would have a hearing with the parole board to see if and when I would be released, and even if they released me, I knew it would take some time before I walked out these prison doors.

Today was that day. I hurried up and got in and out of the shower and put on my "nice" clothes. I had my moms send me some clothes just for this day. It wasn't much but an all white button up shirt, some all black slacks, and some off brand shoes. I sprayed a little cologne that I had in my shower bag and went back to my cell and put my things up. By this time, everyone was getting let out for the morning and on their way to the showers. I hopped on my top bunk and let my feet hang over the sides and rested my head in my hands and said a silent prayer. I didn't know how this day was going to go, but I hoped it played in my favor.

"Los, let's go, big dawg," Mickey said as he appeared at my cell door. I inhaled deeply one last time and hopped off the bed, landing on my two feet.

"Let's do it," I said. He cuffed my wrist in front of me and patrolled me out of my cell and to the office where the hearing would be held. Walking down this long hall that led to another door that we had to walk through, I noticed Sasha standing at attention, trying not to smile at me, but I couldn't contain mine. Mickey was cool, so I wasn't worried about him saying anything. I flashed my pearly whites at her as we made it to her door, and surprisingly, they traded me of,f and it was her who was going to escort me to the office and back to my GP.

"Good luck, inmate," Mickey said as he turned back around headed back to his post.

"Why do you need luck, inmate?" Sasha asked, keeping a straight face.

"My parole hearing. So when I get out of here, we gettin' married, right?" I said as she side eyed me, and I gave her a devilish grin. I could tell that something was a little off because she had yet to say anything about the letter I wrote her, and she looked overly tired.

"Parole hearing, huh? So you 'bout to be a free man soon?" she asked as we rounded the corner and headed to the last room on the left.

"You read my letter yet?" I blatantly asked. Her eyebrows raised, and she got wide-eyed.

"Oh, my goodness, it's in my other pants, and I forgot all about it. I had such a fucked up night after I clocked out, you wouldn't even imagine," she said, looking straight ahead as if we weren't talking.

"Fucked up how?" I asked her as we arrived at the room and waited for them to open it.

"I caught my man fucking my best friend," Sasha said just as the parole members opened the door and escorted me in. I was shocked my damn self at what she just told me, and it was a bit funny. I had to supress my laughter until later, but damn; her best friend, though? Niggas ain't shit.

"Mr. Weston, have a seat," Janice, a white lady, said as I took my seat. There were three workers in the room, and they all had name tags. There was also Rich, an older Caucasian man, and Monice, an older African-American lady that I saw often around the facility. Jeremy, my case manager was also in attendance, sitting at the table as well.

"How are you today?" Janice asked me that stupid question.

"I'm sitting in front of three people that are about to determine my fate, I don't know how I'm doing at the moment, ma'am." I kept it real with her, and she took it that way.

"Understandable," Janice said as she started shuffling through papers and looking through my file.

Janice gave my case manager and I a copy of my case file, and me and him looked it over together. After a couple of minutes of small talk, it was time to start the hearing

"So, Mr. Weston, this hearing is being recorded, as you may know. This hearing is to determine your eligibility for parole. You have served two of the twenty years that you were sentenced to, and we are determining if we will release you earlier than your mandated sentence. Do you or Jeremy have any questions before we start?" Janice asked. Both me and Jeremy said we didn't have any questions at the moment.

"Okay. Let's get started, shall we?" Janice smiled.

"So, with the information we collected about your two year stay so far, unfortunately, we have to deny this hearing. Even though most of your stay here has been incident-free, there was a recent incident in the cafe where a group of inmates were fighting, and even though you weren't physically involved because I know you were detained by one of our guards, your name came up once about being one who orchestrated the hit on the inmate that was stabbed to death, and until we can prove your innocence, you will continue your sentence," Janice said as she sat there and looked from my worker back to me.

"That's bullshit, Commissioner, and you know it!" I stood up and yelled. One of the male guards grabbed me by the shoulder and pushed me back down in my seat.

"Calm down, Carlos, before they send you to SEG, and you definitely won't be getting out any time soon," Jeremy said, looking at me. I sat back in my seat and rubbed my face with my handcuffed hands. I didn't have shit to do with that fight, and I didn't know who said I did, but when I found out who it was, and I was sure I would be finding out, they gon' get that ass beat. I instantly got a headache and hung my head down in between my legs.

"Carlos, I know this may be hard to deal with, but you have

to remain calm because this behavior will only put more time on your sentence, and that's what we're trying to prevent." Rich chimed in. After a couple more minutes of discussing some legal things, the hearing was over. I wasn't in the best mood, so when I was escorted back to GP with Sasha, she sensed something was off.

"You okay?" she asked with sincerity.

"Nope, but I knew this was a possibility," I said shaking my head. The rest of the walk was silent as I didn't even feel like talking. I needed to let out some steam, so when we got back to GP, I walked to the weight room. I took my place at the empty weight bench and laid back. Positioning myself the right way, I started my presses. I noticed that working out for me was a stress reliever, and the bonus was getting my body right. I didn't have a six-pack, but my stomach was flat. My arms were starting to buff, and my chest was starting to get tight. I believed that I favored Lance Gross, with a body like 50 Cent, minus the abs. I closed my eyes as I sped up, making the dumbell hit my chest as I counted. I got to twenty when I felt someone staring at me, so I instantly opened my eyes and saw Mac, one of Meechie's old runners staring me down. I put the bar back in place and sat up, breathing heavily as I caught my breath. He walked up to where I was seated. I quickly stood up because I knew in jail having another man stand over you was a no-no. He stopped in front of me and crossed his arms in front of him.

"Fuck you want, nigga?" I asked, ready to throw them hands.

"I heard you a rat, nigga," Mac said.

"Nigga, fuck you and Meechie!" I spat back at him. I didn't give a fuck about him because wasn't no nigga that bled like me putting fear in my heart.

"You gon' get yours, nigga," Mac said as he nodded his head in a yes motion. As bad as I wanted to knock this big goofy Martin Lawernce-looking muthafucka out, I knew I wanted to be out this joint, so I decided agaisnt it, but if this nigga would have touched me, I would have laid his ass out, and he knew it. Mac and I used to do some running for Meechie, and he saw plenty of times how I was with these hands, so I didn't know why he was trying me.

"Inmates, stand down before I throw both of y'all asses in SEG!" Mickey yelled. At the end of the day, he still had a job to do. I gave Mac a smile and turned around and grabbed my shirt off the floor and threw it over my shoulder.

"You got some more shit to say? Cuz if not, why you still standing here?"

"Yeah, nigga, just know I know what it is, and you know what happens to rats," Mac said as he turned around and walked away.

"Yeah, alright, nigga," I said to his back.

I needed to pull some rank in this muthafucka before I never got out, and I didn't mean walking out the doors, I meant in a body bag. I made up my mind and decided I was going to ask Sasha to be a mule for me until I could get some shit situated, and I hoped she agreed because when niggas knew you held that weight, they knew not to fuck with you, and I needed to stay on the commissioner's good side for the time being, but I was definitly about to get the money flowing in here one way or another.

Chapter 11

Sasha

After a long day at work, I finally made it home and stripped out of my uniform and laid out on my bed. I just laid there for a minute because it seemed like ever since I started this new position, I was at work more than I was home. I was now in a more peaceful place than I had ever been in since I stopped messing with Anthony, and I was happy about that. I rolled over onto my back, and my thoughts instantly went to Carlos and how his demeanor changed once he left out of the parole hearing. Thinking about the letter he gave me that I never read, I jumped up and raced to my uniform pants that I threw in the dirty clothes hamper and went back to my bed. Opening it up, I smiled because it was a turn on for me for men that had good penmanship.

Hey, Gorgeous,

I know I'm not supposed to be doing this, but you're too beautiful for me to just let you pass by. I know this shit is corny as hell, so don't be over there laughing at me and shit, but from the moment we locked eyes I knew you would be mine. Unfortunately, the circumstances that are present is what is making it difficult for you to be mine, and I understand that. A man can't protect and provide behind these four walls and that's all I'm about. If we get a chance, I would love to call and talk to you because I know I can't say much when we see each other because I don't want you to lose your job, and I'm not tryna go to the hole either, but I just had to say something because I felt like we made a kind of weird connection. I don't plan on spending the he rest of my days here in this hell hole, I don't have a support system, I don't have kids or a woman that you have to worry about. By the way, I'm Carlos Weston, they call me Los, but you can call me Big daddy Loster (joking). I would love to connect with you more, so if this kite sits well with you, write me back, and I'm sure you will find a way to get it back to me, and if not, I shot my shot and tried. Love, Los.

I was smiling from ear to ear like a high school kid in love. This just made my stomach flutter and my heart skip a beat. I re-read the letter over and over again until I decided to write him back. I knew how to get the letter back to him, and I planned to do so when I got back to work. Tomorrow was my day off, so I was going to stay in the house all day and do absolutely nothing. I folded the letter back and put it in my jewelry box and laid back down, cuddling with my pillow. I grabbed my remote to my T.V a tuned into Lifetime as a movie was just starting. I grabbed my blunt I rolled before I went to work, lit and smoked it while the movie watched me. As hard as I tried to not think about Carlos, it was hard. Maybe because Anthony broke my heart, and I was naive and vulnerable, or the fact that I hadn't been called beautiful in a very long time, but what ever it was had me all in my feelings. I decided that I was going to write him back and give him my number, but then I thought about it. I didn't want my number to be traced back to anybody in the jail, so I had get another cheap phone or something. I decided when I got up in the morning, I was going to go get one of those cheap prepaid phones from Walmart and put it under a different name and start a Securtel account. In the midst of me daydreaming, my cell phone rang, and like always, I left it in my purse in the kitchen, so I hauled ass out of bed and raced to the phone to see who was calling, and it was Angie from work.

"*Hello,*" I said, damn near out of breath.

"*Hey, bitch, what you doin'?*" she asked sounding straight like one of the sistas.

"*Nothing, girl, sitting here watching TV, smoking, what you doin'?"* I asked her.

"Shit, bored on this Thursday night. The Nineties got dollar drinks tonight, you game?" Even though I didn't want to go anywhere, I did want to throwback a couple Tequila Sunrises. The Nineties was a gay bar that had the strongest drinks and the bombest music. The vibe was always lit at the Nineties, and the more I thought about it, the more I became excited.

"Fuck it, why not?" I said.

"Good, I'ma Uber there because I planned to get intoxicated tonight."

"Shit, I might as well too." I laughed.

"So, did you hear about the fight that almost happened between them two dudes in the weight room?" she asked me.

"Nah, who?" I asked curiously.

"Mac and that fine ass Carlos dude. Girl, they were face to face 'bout to bang it out, but Mickey stopped it," Angie said. I didn't know anything about it. All I knew was when I escorted him back to general population, he was mad as shit. He barely said two words to me which was understandable. I assumed his hearing with the big bosses didn't go too well, so he was mad about that.

"Nah, I didn't hear shit about that," I said as I kept it simple. She was cool and all, but I wasn't going to tell her that me and Carlos were talking.

"Girl, ain't he fine though? I know he slangin' like a damn horse," Angie said about Carlos.

"Yeah, he is fine as fuck," I said. Now, she had me wondering about what he was packing below the shorts, and I was sure it was slanging. Thinking about that had my panties getting a little moist.

"Okay, let me get off this phone and start getting ready. I'll be

there at like ten."

"*Okay, ten is cool,*" I said, and we hung up. It wasn't going to take me that long to get dressed because it was a casual bar, and I planned to be casual. I walked to my closet and grabbed a bag of new clothes I had yet to wear and grabbed a pair of distressed hot pink pants and a onesie type V-neck long sleeved shirt, and I had bought some bomb ass open-toed tan wedges with pink flowers. I picked out my undergarments I was going to wear. It was already seven, so I sat in my bed and set my alarm for nine and laid down to take a nap before the festivities.

My nap ended up being longer and deeper than I thought because when I woke up, it was extremely dark out. I grabbed my phone from under my pillow, and it was nine-fifteen, and I had three missed calls from Angie. I pressed the green button and called her back because I was sure she thought I was going to send her off.

"*Damn, you are alive,*" she said as soon as she answered.

"*My bad, girl, I called myself taking a nap and slept on my phone,*" I said as I walked in my bathroom and started the shower.

"*Bitch, is you still goin', cuz im not going out by myself!*"

"*Yeah, I'm going, I'm hoping in the shower now. I picked out my outfit when we got off the phone, so all I gotta do is shower,*" I said as I stepped out of my clothes. It took me about thirty to shower and get dressed, I applied some eye liner and mascara to my face and some regular lip gloss on my lips and waited for her to get here.

Angie made it to my house by nine-thirty, and I could tell she had already had a drink or three. Hell, I couldn't wait to get on her level, so I went into the liquor cabinet and grabbed my bottle of Patron and went to my glass cabinet and grabbed Angie and I some shot glasses. I filled our shot glasses to the rim and passed Angie hers.

"Toast to getting lit tonight," I said, lifting my drink.

"Toast it up, bitchhhhhh!" Angie yelled.

We took a couple more shots before we called over the Uber which came in like ten minutes. We stood in line for another twenty minutes until we finally reached the check in, and we showed the bouncer our ID's. When we walked in, *Press by Cardi B* was bumping through the speakers, and everyone in the bar was rapping along while holding their drinks. We went straight to the bar, and luckily, no one was ordering, so we were able to grab our drinks and head to the dance floor. Angie ordered a blue muthafucka, and I ordered that to start with as well. Them drinks had a mixture of vodka and would have you lit on your ass if you had too many.

"Ding-Dong, must be the new whip that I ordered, and a new crib for my daughter,
You know a bad bitch gon' spoil her."

We both rapped along and bobbed our heads to the song as we grabbed our drinks and got in the middle of the crowd. After we danced to about five songs and went back to the bar for our second drink and downed that one, we were finally sitting down at an open table and feeling ourselves.

"Bitch, you see that stud kept tryna grab my ass?" Angie asked as she yelled over the music in my ear.

"Girl, I saw her cop a feel a couple times, don't act like you didn't like that shit!" I yelled back at her. Overall, we were enjoying ourselves when someone I didn't expect to see showed up--Brittani. She showed up with a female I'd never seen before, and they both looked ratchet. I nudged Angie and pointed Brittani out to her, and she instantly was TTG.

"What you wanna do, sis?" she asked as she looked at me. Just then, Brittani turned my way and noticed me sitting there staring her down. She gave me a sly smile, and that shit pissed me off. I would rather her mug me than to smile, now I felt like she was taunting me, and I wasn't having that shit. I knew me and her would end up having some words eventually tonight, and lowkey, I was ready to put my hands on her raggedy ass again.

"I'ma let this shit play out, but know if this bitch get beside herself, I'ma put the paws on this nasty hoe," I said with disgust in my face. I was now close to being drunk, and I was starting to get in my feelings. I was supposed to be here with that bitch. I moved up here with this stanky bitch, and she turned around and fucked on my man when I would cry to her about how he dogged me out and how he was playing me with all these bitches, and this bitch was playing the field the whole time. I was legit hurt. Angie must have read my expression because she put her arm around me and told me fuck her and that we were gonna turn up tonight.

We went back to the bar, and I got my last drink of the night because now that she was turned, up I didn't want to be caught slipping, so I got a Tequila Sunrise and a bottled water. Angie was now all up in the stud's face that she was complaining about earlier, and her homegirl was all up in mine. Even though I wasn't into girls, I tended to become bisexual when I was drunk, so I was going with the flow. It was fifteen minutes 'til two, so they started playing all the slow jams, so I decided to dance with the girl I'd been flirting with all night. *Nice and Slow* by Usher was playing, and she pulled me in and grabbed my waist. I sang along to the song as we swayed back and forth when someone pushed me so hard, I fell into her, and she stumbled back. I looked back, and Brittani's drunk ass nudged me and kept walking like nothing happened.

I looked over at Angie who saw what had gone down, and she saw the look on my face and knew it was game time. I was waiting for this bitch to jump stupid, and she did it at the right time. I went after her, which she was now speed walking out the club, and when I caught up to her, I grabbed her by her shirt, and she spun around. We looked at each other for a second, and anger overcame me, and I punched her dead in her face. She stumbled backwards but didn't fall, and I went in for some more.

"Bitch, I hate yo conniving ass!" I said as we started throwing haymakers at each other. It was like we were in a wrestling match with no ref. The bouncers were now pulling us apart, and I got the last kick in, which landed on her side. We were already by the entrance, so they carried us a couple feet to the door and watched us walk out. Me and Angie went one way, and Brittani and her friend went the other way.

"Bitch, you was handling her ass," Angie said as we went to the bus stop across the street and sat on the bench as I ordered the Uber. It was two minutes away, so we stood at the curb and looked out for the black Nissan. Angie ended up coming with me to my house because she didn't want to take an Uber home drunk by herself which was understandable, and when we made it to the house, we were both drunk as fuck. It always seemed like the ride home was the worst when you out drinking because that's when your liquor settles in because you're not moving and dancing around anymore. Angie fell out on the couch, and I stumbled to go get her a blanket and pillow from out the hall closet, and by the time I got back, she was snoring drunk sleep. I was drunk my damn self and damn near crawled to my bed. I took all my clothes off and got under my blanket butt ass naked.

The next morning, I woke up with a slight headache, but no hangover surprisingly. I could still taste the vodka in my mouth from last night, and my makeup was smeared on my pillow case, so I knew it was a good night. I slowly crawled out of bed and wrapped my throw blanket around my body and walked to the living room to check on Angie. When I walked in and saw she wasn't on the couch, but there was a note. I read the

RISKING IT ALL FOR A CONVICT

note, and it simply said that I was out cold and that she called an Uber and went home. I locked my door and walked back to the room and got my phone to text Angie to see if she made it home safe. When she replied, I put my phone on the charger and went into the bathroom to get this alcohol off my breath and out of my pores with a nice hot shower. I didn't have much on my agenda today but to get some groceries and go to Walmart to get the prepaid phone I needed.

I wrote the letter that I was going to give to Los when I got to work tomorrow, so all I needed to do was add the number at the bottom and fold it up. When I finally got out the shower and dressed, I got in my car and drove to Walmart which was only about ten minutes from my house, and I was in and out. I purposely only bought a set amount of money out with me because I tended to go crazy in Walmart, buying unnecessary shit, so I only took the amount of money that I needed. When I left out of Wally World, as some people called it, I walked over to Starbucks and grabbed me a strawberry and creme drink and a bagel with cream cheese. I had eaten the whole thing before I even pulled out of the parking lot while I sat and scrolled down Instagram. I hooked my phone to my Bluetooth and decided to pull out, when I saw my second mom, Brittani's mom, coming out the store with her new man. I hadn't seen her in about a year, so I was ecstatic when I saw her coming out the door.

"Mommy!" I yelled out while I got out the car. She looked towards me, and a smile instantly formed across her face.

"Hi, my sweetest," she said as we hugged each other, rocking back and forth. "You ain't been comin' to see me," she said. An instant regret formed over me.

"I know, Ma, I been going through it so heavy lately. I'm just now finding my peace," I said honestly, and I was. This last year had been hard for me physically, mentally, and emotionally, but after cutting the two toxic people out of my life, I generally found myself in a better place.

"Yeah, I heard about what happened with my trifling ass child. You gotta forgive her and move forward. Don't let her steal your joy or happiness. That girl is a hot ass mess. I'm glad one of yall making something out of nothing," Ms. Kay said to me sincerely. We talked for another ten minutes before her man said he had to go, so we exchanged hugs one more time, and I got back in my car and pulled off.

When I pulled up to my house, I had a bouquet of flowers on my doorstep, and I thought it was from Anthony. I got out my car disgruntled and made my way to the door.

"This nigga not 'bout to do this. I don't know what the fuck he think this gon' do," I said as I bent down and picked the flowers up, taking the card out to see what bullshit he had them write in it before I threw it out.

To the beautiful, Sasha, may your life be filled with many blessings. I hope to spend time with you and show you what a real man is like.

Sincerely, Daddy Loster.

My heart smiled so big, I just stood on the porch and reread the letter a couple times before I unlocked the door and headed in. I had never received flowers in my life, even with me having a man for five years. I didn't know what it was about this inmate, but I told myself that I wouldn't cross this boundary that I had already crossed. I sat the flowers down in the middle of my coffee table and slipped out of my pants and bra, leaving me with nothing on but my shirt. I sat on the couch and turned my T.V on and let it watch me once again while I stared at my roses. I wondered how this man got my address, but I had an idea. Mickey wanna-be hood ass. I knew them two talked a lot, and I had a feeling he talked him into finding out what my address was in exchange for something. For now, I sat back and relaxed and prepared for my work day tomorrow. I couldn't wait to see

Daddy Los.

Chapter 12

Sasha

The following day, I woke up to a knock on the door. I looked at the clock, and it was only nine in the morning. I was working the second shift today, so I didn't have to be at work until two in the afternoon, so I had no clue to who was at my door so damn early. I crawled out of bed and put on my purple robe and matching slippers to go with them and walked to the door. I looked out the peep hole and saw an older white male with a clipboard in his hand standing on the other side. I put the chain on the door and opened it slightly.

"Yes?" I said as I peeked through a slit in the door.

"Sasha Reynolds?" he asked as he looked at me through the same slit in the door.

"Who's asking?" I asked, now curious to know how he knew my name.

"Are you confirming you're Sasha Reynolds, ma'am?"

"Yes, who are you?" I asked again, now becoming a little agitated. He pulled out a white envelope and stuck it through the door for me to grab.

"You've been served. Have a great day. Sorry for waking you," he said as he tipped his hat to me and walked off.

"The fuck?" I said to myself as I hurried and closed my door and made my way back to my bedroom and ripped the envelope open like I was receiving a check. As I read over the letter my stomach started to form in knots. I was getting evicted. It said that the rent hadn't been paid in almost two months, and I didn't understand how that would have happened because the last time I spoke with Anthony, he agreed to handle the rent until the lease was up in two months.. I was now pissed and flew over my bed and grabbed my phone that was on the nightstand. Even though I deleted his number, I dialed it on the pad because I remembered it by heart. The phone rang a couple times and went straight to voicemail.

"Not today, bitch," I said as I called again. I didn't know what he thought, but Anthony was about to answer this phone today. I called three more times before he picked up, and when he didn't, my anger rose through the roof in two seconds because I heard Brittani in the background asking why I was calling.

"*Yes, Sash?*" Anthony asked as if I was bothering him or something.

"*So, the agreement was that you were going to help pay the rent until the lease was up, and now I see you had a change of heart. Did you decide against telling me?*" I said not giving a fuck about that bitch being in her feelings while I spoke to the man she called herself stealing from me.

"*I'm not living there no more, so why do I have to pay the rent, Sash?*" he asked me.

"*Nigga, you not living here no more because you wanted that skank ass bitch so bad, now you got her. That's not what I called for. I got subpoenaed today, so you haven't paid her in two months, and you knew that, and you was just gon' let me get put out on the street, nigga? After you just showed up to my job not too long ago begging me for forgiveness, and you knew I would be getting put out?*" I asked him, now starting to get in my feelings a little bit. Niggas could front they moved all day and still turn around and play you like it was nothing.

"*You went to her job, AT?*" I heard Brittani ask Anthony.

"*Oh, so she got in good enough to call you AT now? I guess y'all got well acquainted, huh, my nigga? You could have at least told me you wasn't gon' pay it, that's all I'm getting at! You know what, fuck you, Anthony. I'ma figure the shit out. I hope you rot in hell, bitch ass nigga,*" I said as I hung the phone up and blocked his number. I went and scrolled through my contact info and dialed my goofy ass landlord's number, and of course, she didn't answer. She knew what transpired between Anthony and I, so why she didn't come to me before she took this shit to court baffled me. I threw my phone to the side, and it slid off the bed and onto the floor, and I laid back on my bed and sat in deep thought for a second. I literally had no one to turn to now, and that was getting to me. I tried to think of everything possible that I could do to get the sixteen hundred in rent that was due in a week since I didn't get my next check for another two weeks. After refurbishing the house and paying my car note and the little bills we did share around the house, I was broke already, and I was due in court in seven days. I prayed that they would throw me a break and give me a grace period of when I could pay it, but being that this wasn't the first time we were late on rent, I highly doubted that they would show me any leniency.

My mind was racing a mile a minute, so I got out of bed and grabbed my Mary Jane off the dresser and rolled me a blunt. It was nearing ten in the morning, and I still had time to myself, so I turned on my radio and decided to straighten up a bit to clear my head as I smoked. I put a load of clothes mixed with my uniform in the washer and clean the kitchen and bathroom and vacuumed my rugs. After all that was done, it was about twelve-thirty, and I got in the shower as my clothes were drying.

At that moment, I felt like I had hit my lowest and let it all come out. I cried like a baby as the hot water ran down my body. I only could blame myself because I didn't know why I thought this nigga would keep his word. Hell, he didn't do what he said he would when he was here. After my shower, I got dressed and walked out the door and headed to work. I had to put my big girl panties on and figure some shit out and quick, or I would be out here homeless, and I wasn't going for that. The whole way to work was very bland. I made it to work quicker than usual, parked in the designated parking spot, and got out the car. I normally sat and scrolled through social media, but today I just wanted to get this day over with.

After I clocked in and put my things up, I walked to the lead officer and got an overview on how everything was going on the floor and got the shift change report. After I was done with that, I walked the floors to check on everyone and went back to my designated post until it was my time to walk the floor and check on the inmates. I took my seat behind the counter and watched the cameras for about an hour before Angie showed up and sat next to me. I had forgotten that she was scheduled to work with me tonight, so when she showed up, I knew tonight's shift was going to go by fun and quick. Angie was a thick ass white girl that had to grow up in the hood somewhere. We weren't that close as of yet, so I didn't really know that much about her besides she only dated black men because that's all she ever talked about. I felt like if you squinted hard enough, she looked and acted like the teenage viral sensation Woah Vicky, but a little older. She had hips and ass like a sister with a thick waist like me, and I was almost a sixteen in pants.

"Hey, boo," she said as she sat down and did a three-sixty spin in her chair before she turned her cameras on, on her computer

"Wassup, boo? You're late," I said, smiling at her because I knew she was high as a kite. Her eyes were low and a bit pink, but to a non-smoker, it could easily look like she was tired or had been crying.

"I know. I had to handle some business, if you know what I mean," she said cheesing and honestly, I didn't know what she meant.

"What business you gotta handle at work, girl?" I asked her.

"Business, baby," she said, giving me a side smirk. I guess that was my cue to mind my damn business, and I didn't ask her about it no more. After talking with her for a couple minutes about our night going out and how she had a hangover when she got home the morning after leaving my house, it was time for me to walk the floor. I felt against my pocket and made sure my letter was there and folded tightly I started my rounds for the night. I typically didn't see Los until I did cell check and lock up, and my stomach was fluttering with butterflies. For some reason, I couldn't wait until I got to see his face and give him this letter because after today, he would have access to call me, and we could get to know each other on a better level than when we passed each other or had a quick thirty-second conversation. I walked the bottom floor first before I headed upstairs. I didn't like this floor at all because I always got harassed by the inmates. There was this one black man that was in here for the rest of his life, and he just didn't give a fuck what he said or what he did. I guess he said his life was over anyway, so why not show out? When I walked by his cell, he instantly stood up and came to the door. It wasn't yet time for lock up, so the doors were still open.

"Hey, girl," he said to me as he stood, leaning on the cell door frame, grabbing his dick with his left hand and playing around with a toothpick in his right hand.

"Officer Sasha works better than hey girl, what you need, inmate?" I asked him, demanding authority at the same time.

"Why don't you come in for a couple seconds, let me show you something," he said to me with a smirk on his face. Without stepping a foot towards him, I stood where I was at and told him about himself.

"Look ,inmate, either you stop with this bullshit, or

you're going to be reported. I would advise you to stop fucking playing with me before I make you swallow that damn toothpick. You have been warned. The next time you let some slick shit come out your lips toward me, I'll make sure the warden hears about it. That would be strike three, right?" I asked him, giving him the 'stop fucking playing with me' look.

"Okay, guard," he responded as he turned around slowly and headed back into his cell.

I shook my head and kept it moving. That's one thing that I learned, you had to have thick skin with these males, and I tried my best to let them know I wasn't the one to fuck with. I kept it moving, looking in each cell, making sure they weren't doing anything they weren't supposed to be doing until I got to the last cell on the bottom floor. When I noticed that they had a look out watching to see when I got down there, it made me speed up a bit to see what they were doing in there that they had to look out for me. I got closer to the cell and smelled tobacco and burning paper. These white boys were smoking a cigarette that they rolled in a piece of regular writing paper. The lookout turned quickly and went back into his cell, and when I made it to the door, it was about four of them looking like a deer caught in the headlights. I used my walkie talkie and asked for assistance and sent them my location because I wasn't going to enter the cell by myself. It took my co-workers about thirty seconds to reach me, and we entered the cell. Pulling each inmate out and escorting them to the wall, I handcuffed all four of them and sat them on the floor. Mickey, which was one of the guards that came to my aide, said something in his walkie, and the lock up alarm sounded, letting all the inmates know it was time to close all cell doors except the one we were about to search.

While one of my co-workers stood out and kept an eye on the inmates that were cuffed, we got to destroying the cell to find the rest of the tobacco. This was the part I liked and disliked at the same time because I felt like these were their homes, and we had to pull everything from everywhere, purposely to find what we were looking for, and they were left with the hassle of cleaning our mess, but oh well. I guess that's what happened when you came to jail; you had no privacy. After about an hour of searching, we found a small bag of tobacco and a man-made shank that looked like it had been used because it had dried blood on it. Everything we collected was put in a collection bag and turned in, and the individuals that were handcuffed were sent to SEG until they were dealt with. I had to write a report on what I had seen and everything that took place within the situation and turned it into my the review board also.

That incident took an extra hour out of my time, so I hoped no one walked the second floor for me because I wanted to at least see his face before my shift ended. After being told that I still had to walk the upper floor, I proceeded to do just that. Due to having to lock the doors because of contraband being found, all inmates were off the floor. I went and checked each cell door and made sure they were locked, I also looked inside to see what they were doing. Being that I was a female, a cute one at that, I heard derogatory comments almost all day every day, and tonight was no different.

The first cell that I looked in, one of the inmates was licking his tongue at me, and the next cell one of the inmates was making a gesture as if he was fucking someone from the back. They weren't doing anything out of the ordinary nor were they physically saying anything to me, so I let them do what they were doing and kept it moving. I looked around the unit and made sure that everyone was in their cells and the other guards weren't around because I was approaching Carlos' cell. I got to his door and looked through the window, and he was smiling so hard at me that I couldn't help but smile back. He walked up the door and slipped a small folded up letter through the slit. I didn't want to stay at his door too long, so I quickly slipped my letter in the small slit in the door, gave him a smile, and kept it moving. Normally, when we saw a small nick anywhere, we were supposed to tell someone about it, but being that it was beneficial for me at the moment, I was going to keep that a little secret. That man gave me butterflies, and I didn't know why. His white teeth were like a ray of sunshine for me. Sometimes I felt silly for having feelings for an inmate, let alone one that I only come in contact with maybe once a day if that.

When I was done checking on the inmates, I walked back to the desk and sat down. I rested my head on the headrest on the chair and exhaled deeply. Tonight had been one of those stressful and long nights, and I just couldn't wait to get home, smoke me a blunt, and call it a night. Angie was still posted watching the cameras, so when I sat down, of course, she wanted to know what went down. I told her what had happened, and she laughed it off. Angie actually liked the cat calls and nasty comments that the inmates made to her, and instead of her correcting the issue, she smiles at them and said little shit back. Yes, who was I to be talking when I was feeling Carlos? But that's different. He didn't approach me how these inmates approached her, and being that she had a man walking amongst the same men she flirted with in return just made for a disaster waiting to happen. It was almost midnight and time for a shift change, so I started doing my paperwork for the night and had one last round to do before I clocked out. I saw Mickey coming down the hall and decided to see if he was the one that ordered the flowers for Los to be sent to my house and how he got a hold of my address.

"Hey, Mickey, let me talk to you for a second," I said as I got out of my chair and walked around the counter to where he was walking to.

"What's up, Sasha?" he asked giving me a smile. Mickey was a cool ass white boy who knew the ends and outs of this jail, so that's why I knew it was him and because I saw he and Carlos had a bond going on.

"Did you have something delivered to my house for an inmate?" I asked flat out.

"Yes, he wanted flowers sent to your house and paid me a little something, something to dig up your address and send it," Mickey said as he looked at me with his blue eyes. Sometimes I wondered if Mickey had a thing for me because he tried to flirt sometimes, and I just let it go over my head. I liked my meat well done.

"So, you just do what the inmates say? What if I didn't want no flowers?" I asked him to give him the black girl's stance, putting my hand on my hip and cocking my neck.

"From what I already heard, he bagged and tagged you. Don't fake it like you ain't feeling Los. He a good dude and heard he supposed to be getting out soon," he said, looking at me up and down, like he was undressing me with his eyes.

"He ain't bag and tag shit. Don't do that shit again," I said, poking him in the chest and returning back to my seat. It made me nervous and happy at the same time because if word was getting around that he bagged and tagged me as Mickey put it, I didn't want to be caught and lose my job. That had me reconsidering even entertaining Carlos.

"What y'all was talkin' about?" Angie asked me looking curious.

"Business. Ain't that how you put it?" I asked her, referring back to her vague answer she gave earlier.

"Hmmm," she said, sounding a little salty. It was now time to clock out, and I damn near ran back to the employee lounge to punch out. It took me about ten minutes from the time I was at the cameras to clock out and get in my car. I was tired and just wanted to go home and read the letter my boo wrote and hope that he called tomorrow, which I was sure he would. I made it home in about twenty minutes and was ready to strip and relax in my king size bed. I grabbed my purse out the passenger seat and grabbed my phone out the console and walked to my door.

As I put my keys in the door, I heard someone whistle at me. I jumped and turned around to see if I saw anyone, and I didn't. I hurried up and fumbled with my keys again and turned the lock. As I opened my door, I felt someone push me into the house and came in with me. I turned to see who it was, and of course, it was Anthony.

"What the fuck is wrong with you?" I asked him, my voice a bit shaken. He turned and locked the door and grabbed my purse off the floor that fell when he pushed me in the door. He grabbed my phone and keys and threw them across the room, and that worried me. I took a second look at him, and I could tell that he was drunk, and I knew how tonight was going to go. At that instant, I remembered that I bought a small deuce five and put it in the chest that was sitting in the hall next to the front door just in case of emergencies like this.

"So, who you think you call being all tough this morning, Sasha?" Anthony asked as he started walking toward me. I stood up and tried to maneuver around him to get closer to the chest that was about three feet away from me, but he was too quick. He grabbed me by my neck and flung me into the living room. I fell against the couch and bounced back up. I wasn't going to let him whoop my ass without a fight. It was like he was in a blind rage, and nothing I would say would snap him out of it.

"Anthony, get the fuck out. I don't want to do this with you tonight," I said as I circled my living room table. It was like we were playing ring around the rosie or something. He lunged over the table and tried to grab me and lost his balance, falling over it. I jumped back and realized I had some seconds to reach my gun, and that was exactly what I did. I ran into the hall back by the door and flung the top of the chest open and grabbed the gun that was laying on top of all the mess I had in there. Anthony got up from the table and stumbled in the hall where I was.

"You take another step towards me, I'll flat line yo ass, nigga," I said, pointing the gun directly at his face. He looked at me, and his eyes widened when he saw I was aiming at his head. He knew it was real because he was the one that taught me how to shoot, so he knew what it was.

"So, you pullin' a gun out on me, Sasha, that's how you feel?" Anthony questioned as he took another step towards me, and I cocked my pistol back. At that moment, I didn't know what I was going to do, but I wasn't going to let him put his hands on me anymore.

"You think I'm 'bout to sit here and let you whoop my ass? Nah, we past that shit. Not no more," I said, shaking my head, answering myself more than talking to him. I was looking Anthony directly in his eyes to let him know I wasn't playing. Hell, I worked with niggas harder than his pussy ass all day, and I didn't take no shit from them, so I was definitely not gon' take it from him anymore. If anything, I'd use what I learned while I was training and hit one of his pressure points and kick his ass while he was drunk, but I didn't feel like stretching the situation out, so this would do for now.

"Okay, Sasha. You won, mami. I'ma get up out yo shit," Anthony said as he laughed to himself and stumbled towards the door. I heard him mumbling something under his breath but couldn't make it out, so I let it be. Anthony fumbled with my door handle and locks until he finally got the door open and walked out without saying another word. I ran to the door and locked it quickly and pushed the heavy chest that I got my gun out of in front of the door just in case he had a change of heart and wanted to come back. My emotions were all over the place, and all I could do was weep to myself.

I walked backwards until my body hit the wall next to the living room, and I slid down, my butt hitting the floor harder than I would have liked. I sat in place and slid the gun on the other side of the room. Resting my head on the wall, I sighed deeply. This was the third time that Anthony had put his hand on me in the five years we were dating, and those incidents happened at the beginning of our relationship, so I didn't know what was going on in his mind tonight. I knew the conversation earlier was a little tense but not enough to try and beat my ass. It was like at that instant, I felt at my lowest because all my life hurdles were being thrown to me at once. From me getting evicted, to my man and best friend fucking, to this new crush that I had that I shouldn't even be having was all too much.

Thinking of Carlos, I reached in my pocket and felt the letter that he wrote to me. I didn't know what made me want to read the letter at that moment, but something told me to. I got myself up and started unfolding the letter as I slowly walked to my room. I put the letter on the dresser and undressed from head to toe and started to crawl into my bed when I decided it would be a good idea to get the gun and have it near me just in case he decided he was going to pop back up. After grabbing it from the hall, I walked back into my room, grabbed the letter, and got under my blankets. My body instantly became one with my mattress as the sheets were nice and cool, and I had one of those big fluffy blankets and that felt good against my bear skin. I started reading the letter and instantly started smiling. It was like he was sweet and corny at the same time, and it made my insides smile. I continued on reading, and he was just telling me about himself and how he hoped his appeal was granted, but it was the last part of the letter that caught my eye. He stated that Mickey was the one that sent me the flowers for him because he owed him a favor.

The letter said that Mickey was doing drops for him in ex change for some money, and Mickey all of a sudden told him he didn't want to do it anymore, and he wanted to keep his money flowing in. Carlos was basically asking me if I could become his mule from the outside. I bring him drugs in the inside, and someone on the outside pays me. I put his portion up and take my portion out. It all seemed so simple when it was said like that, but the process wasn't as simple as I thought it would be. I had to think on this very hard because it was like temptation being in the situation I was just put in about my rent. I folded the letter and put it in my nightstand drawer and made my way to the shower. I had a long night and was ready to lay it down. I had a lot on my mind, and I had to think about what I was going to do.

Chapter 13

Sasha

Eventually, I made up my mind to get that quick money and bring some weed inside the prison walls for my boo. It had been three months since I did my first drop and six months since I'd been employed at Hennepin County. When I first did my drop, I was a nervous wreck, but the rent was due, and I didn't have another way to get the money quickly. Carlos had contacted me and told me that he had someone that would bring me a nice eighth of weed and show me how to bag it in smaller portions so it would be easier to get in and conceal. I thought I was going to meet with a nigga that looked like he sold drugs, but to my surprise, it was a white woman that looked like she was in her mid-forties and never touched a drug a day in her life. She was nicer than I thought and when she was showing me how to bag it up. She made sure I understood what I was doing and what I was getting myself into. After her helping me bag it up the first couple times, I was on my own, and I was comfortable with that. She started just dropping it off to me or leaving it in my mailbox.

When it came to bagging the weed up, I would weigh it out on the scale I bought from the local corner store, and I would weigh out half a gram which was point five and put it in a small balloon. I would make sure it was tied tightly and cut the loose end and burn it to ensure it wouldn't untie and the product wouldn't come out. I did that with the rest of the weed until there was no more. When it was time to do the drop, I put the small weed bags inside a non-lubricated condom and tied it tightly, then I would stick it up my kitty. When I got to work,

VELLE B.

I would go to the basement floor bathroom where Black Zack, one of the inmates that was cool with Los and also worked as a janitor at night, would clean the bathroom, and I would leave it inside one of the toilet seats in one of the stalls that were out of order. The first time wasn't as bad as I thought it would be because I was dropping on a floor that no one was barely on, but when the location changed, that's when I became more nervous because we were now putting the product in a more public bathroom, but Carlos reassured me there was nothing to worry about. After he sold all the weed to the other inmates, someone they knew would Cash App, Paypal, or meet up with me and give me the cash that was owed to Los, and I would put his cut up and keep mine.

After the letter that I gave Los with my burner phone number on it, he called me all day and night except the days I was at work. We talked as much as we could whenever we could, and that was the start of the relationship that we now had. We sat on the phone and talked about our goals and dreams, what his plans were when he got out and what his plans were for us once he got out. Our bond was getting tighter and I was really digging that. I caught myself thinking about him a lot throughout my day and even at night. I couldn't wait until I was able to lay in his arms and feel protected. I couldn't wait to feel his big dick inside of my guts, and yes, I knew it was big because when I walked past his cell one day, he had his pants down to his ankles, letting it hang all out, and when I say hang, that's what exactly what it was doing, hanging. It was long and thick and had a curve to it. Sometimes I caught myself fantasizing about him and his third leg. I let him know up front that I was going to keep my guards up with him until he got out and showed me he was different. I didn't let the fact that he was in jail determine if he was a good man or not. Honestly, he was a better man than any man that I'd ever been with, including Anthony. Speaking of Anthony, he tried apologizing numerous times after his drunken incident, even going as far as to send me flowers and cards, having his boys call me and tell me to unblock his number, but I wasn't trying to hear none of that. I was making enough money to move out the place me and Anthony used to share and get another apartment so I could officially move on. Ever since me and Anthony officially stopped all forms of communication, my days had gotten brighter. I was truly in a state of peace and was feeling myself all over again.

It was a Friday night, and I had the following day off. I worked a morning shift, so I was off and at home by five in the evening. I decided that I was going to get some wine and watch a funny movie until my baby gave me a call before they got locked down for the night. It was about eight o'clock, and last call was at ten, so I popped open the Sangria that I had in the fridge and lit the blunt that I had in the ashtray and vibed out. I guess the wine had gotten to me quicker than I thought it would because after my first two cups, I was now in my feelings thinking about my life. My stomach started to turn into knots when I started to think about the people in my life and the people that were supposed to be in my life, and I couldn't help but shed some tears. I hated how people could cross you so bad and not even bat an eye. I started to think about my mother who I hadn't spoken to in almost six years, and that gave me a weary feeling. She hadn't tried to reach out to me either, so I guess I wasn't bothered by it, but now sitting here with an intoxicated brain, I was pissed off.

She allowed her teenage daughter to move halfway across the world with another woman and her child and not call, send a letter, or anything. She didn't know how I was doing, where I was, or how my life was going at the moment, but I always caught myself thinking about her. I was the only child, so I couldn't see how she just didn't give a fuck. Something in my head was telling me to call her to see if she still had the same number, but if I did, what would I say? I missed the first half of the movie I was watching because I was consumed with my thoughts, and that's how I normally got when I drank by myself.

I got out of my bed and walked to my dresser and looked at myself in the mirror. My vision was a little blurred, and I laughed at myself for being tipsy. My hands clutched the edges of the dresser as I put my head down and thought about if I was actually going to call her. Fuck it. She was the person that birthed me, and I deserved some answers. A part of me was hoping that she didn't answer or that the phone number was no longer in service so I wouldn't have to face my reality, but I knew I would have to sooner or later, so why not when I was drunk?

I took a big sip of the wine and sat back on my bed and dialed her number. Before I pressed the dial button, I sat and stared at the phone still contemplating this decision, but it was like my fingers had a mind of their own and pressed the talk button. To my surprise, the phone rang, and my heart started to race. It was now or never because I knew she wouldn't make the first move.

"Hello," a groggy Tanya answered the phone, I could tell that I woke her up.

"Hello?" she repeated. I didn't know why the words couldn't come out of my mouth, but it was like I became mute for a second. It sounded like she let the cigarettes consume her body because her voice was now a little raspier than I remembered.

"Hell-hello?" I said in a low tone, stuttering a bit.

"Um... hello? How many times we gon' say hello? Who is this?" she asked, starting to get agitated. I smirked at myself because I could tell she was still like her attitude having self.

"It's me, Mom," I said as I started fidgeting with the now empty wine glass. The line grew silent as I let what I just said process through her mind before I started talking again.

"Sasha?" Tanya said, sounding surprised. I could tell that she was now up and alert.

"Yes," I responded, not knowing what else to say. There was a long pause before she finally spoke again.

"My goodness. Hi, baby, oh my goodness," she kept saying. In a way, it sounded like she was happy to hear from me and shocked at the same time.

"How you doin', Mama?" I asked her. All the emotions that I knew I was going to have came rushing over me at once, and I almost started tearing up.

"I'm OK, baby. I can't believe you're calling me. I didn't think you ever wanted to talk to me again," Tanya said.

"I didn't think I would either, maybe it's because I have been drinking," I admitted. I laughed a little, and she laughed as well.

"What you drinkin', Mookie?" she asked, calling me by the nickname she used to call me when I was younger. That brought back memories of the time we were happy, and our relationship was good.

"Sangria wine. How's life?" I started to get angry because as much as I wanted to hate her I couldn't. She was still my mom, and a part of me still wanted that bond that we should have had. Was I ready to forgive her? I wasn't sure yet, but I was ready to try.

"Awe, that's my drink!" she said, sounding excited. *"Life is treating me as good as it will get. I can complain about a lot, but I know this phone call will help me get back to where I need to be,"* she said. The conversation went on about how I was doing and what I had going on in my life at the moment, and I asked her the same. We talked for about forty-five minutes about everything under the sun except for what really mattered, and that was why. I had so many questions as to why she did me the way that she did, but the vibe was just going so good that I didn't want to ruin it. I knew that deep down inside she knew that the questions were coming, and I was sure she was glad I chose not

to bring them up, but I hoped that she knew they would be coming within our next couple conversations because believe it or not, I planned to keep connected. We laughed and we joked the whole time, and it honestly felt good. I looked at the clock and noticed it was close to ten, and baby would be calling soon, so I wrapped it up with Mom and told her I would call her when I got up in the morning. It was like clock-work because as soon as I hung up, Carlos was calling me. I answered the phone and pressed zero like the operator told me to do and waited until he clicked through.

"Whaddup, lil' baby?" his low, baritone voice sang through the phone. It was like his voice soothed my ear drums and tingled my insides.

"Hey, big daddy, I miss you," I sang into the phone, cheesing hard, my words slurring just a bit.

"Awe, shit, somebody had something to drink," Carlos said, chuckling a little.

"Yes, I damn near just drunk this whole bottle of wine I told you I bought a couple days ago."

"I see. How your day off goin'? I can't wait to see your beautiful face."

I always thought he sounded like Kevin Gates and told him that multiple times, and it made him blush every time.

"It's goin' good. Just sitting here relaxing. Guess what?"

"Wassup, baby?"

"I called my mom," I told Carlos.

"For real? What happened? Well, why, I'm not tryna be rude, but what made you call her?" he asked me curiously.

"The wine made me call her. I started drinking then started thinking and got in my feelings a little bit and decided to take the initiative and go for it," I said honestly.

"Damn, baby. I'm proud of you for that. It takes a strong woman to do what you did after how she did you. That's some boss shit, boo," Los said. I started to feel better after I talked to him about it, and he told me there's nothing wrong with wanting the love from your mother.

"Thank you, baby. How your night goin'? You was being good today?" I asked, concerned like usual, and per usual he put my nerves to rest.

"I'm always good, baby. I ain't worried 'bout shit. Did all my brothers get you the money to put up for me?" he asked, speaking in code for collecting money from the inmates' family or friends for the debt they owed Carlos.

"No, boo. Eazy didn't bring it to me nor did he call or anything. I'll call him in the morning and see when he can drop it off to me," I said, basically telling Los that Eazy, who Los fronted weed for, his people still hadn't brought me the money that he was promising Los would come. The line grew quiet, and I knew Los was mad as hell.

"Baby, I don't want you to be mad and shit. Remember we are trying to get you out, not keep you in there," I said truthfully. Didn't nobody have time for all that extra shit. He better sit his ass down somewhere because if he got more time put on, I was going to be pissed.

"Carlos, do you hear me?" I asked him when he didn't respond to what I said.

"Mmmhmm," Los mumbled.

"Nah, fuck a mmhmm. Don't play with me, Carlos," I said, getting mad now.

"I hear you, ma, damn," Carlos said aggressively.

"I'ma call you in the morning, boo."

"Carlos, we still got time on the phone," I said, trying to keep

him on the phone, at least until I knew he was calmer, but that didn't work.

"*Nah. I'ma call in the morning. I'm good, my queen; don't trip. I'ma call you as soon as we get out.*"

"*Okay, boo.*"

"*I got love for you, mamas,*" Carlos said in the low voice he knew I loved to hear.

"*I got love for you, too, boo,*" I responded, and he hung up. That was our way of expressing how much we actually cared for each other but not quite in love yet. I couldn't help but smile as I thought about Carlos. Man, he didn't know what he did to me, and as a woman that finally had someone that could make her feel good inside and out, and not even had been touched once, was a wonderful feeling.

Chapter 14

Carlos

After my hearing went south with the parole board, I didn't feel like being bothered with anyone. I didn't have my niggas holding me down like they said they would. My family turned their back on me, the bitches I had when I first came in this muthafucka turned on me too, so the only person that I had to look after me was me. I was emotionally drained at this point. I had been locked up for two years, and the way things were looking, I wasn't getting out any time soon. Every now and then I would call my cousin, Bud, and he would hit my books whenever I needed him too and give me the encouraging words that I needed to hear to keep me sane in a place where the devil was always on my back. Sasha and I had been rocking harder than I thought we would, and that gave me an ounce of hope, but in reality, I didn't know if and when I would be getting out, so I knew not to get my hopes up with her. At the end of the day, I knew she was a woman with needs and dealing with a nigga that was facing years in prison couldn't do her much good, so it would be understandable for her to up and bounce at any second. For the most part, she'd been holding a nigga down as much as she could without jeopardizing herself in the process.

A nigga could get in his feelings real quick when it came to being in prison, especially when it came to a nigga like Mac. That man was trying the fuck out of me, and I couldn't afford to get in no more trouble. I didn't know how he knew about me ratting on Meechie, but he did, and he had been trying to blackmail me for the longest, and I hadn't been paying him too much attention, but I knew if he did actually start telling folks my business, that would create a target on my back and extra problems that I didn't need at the moment.

It was early in the morning, and the doors hadn't opened for the day, so I was in deep thought. I had to deal with Eazy today because this was the second time I gave him some green and his people hasn't paid up yet, so he was going to up all the commissary that he had if his people hadn't paid by the end of the day. Today, he was getting that ass whooped. I hated that I had to jeopardize my freedom this way, but shit, I couldn't let him walk around like shit was good when he knew he owed a debt. I started to become a little restless, so I hopped off the top bunk and decided I was going to get my workout in for the day. I hadn't been going to the weight room as much because I didn't want none of them niggas to catch me slipping. I did a round of push ups, sit ups, and planks for about twenty minutes before I wore myself out. My mind kept going back to the conversation I had with Sasha last night about how she finally spoke with her mother after years of not having any contact with her, and that made me think about my moms and how I hadn't heard from her since I got locked up. I thought about giving her a call, but the thought of rejection made me second guess calling her. My mom had kept in contact with me the beginning of my lock up, and that conversation was just her telling me I needed to grow up and get myself together.

I started getting a little light-headed as I tried to hold my plank longer than I normally did, so I decided to end my work out after about thirty minutes.

I heard the guard's key jiggling as he walked down the hall, so I knew they were about to let us out for the day, and I decided that I was going to handle my business first and let Eazy know it was time to pay up. I wasn't showering today, so I just washed up at my little sink/toilet that was in my cell and called it a day. I grabbed my mini shank that I had made out of an old toothbrush that I sharpened a couple months ago and wrapped it with some old shoe strings that I had and tucked it inside a slit in my boxers that I created in order to keep it in place and waited for the doors to slide open. When they finally opened, I shot out the cell and headed downstairs to Eazy's cell where I knew he would be. When you knew you would be locked down for a long time, you started to notice everything and everybody. I started people watching and being more aware of my surroundings, and I started seeing how most inmates moved, especially the ones that I talked to on a daily.

I walked up to my nigga, Dez, who I grew close with over time, and I told him to be my look out, and he followed me to Eazy's cell. I didn't have to say much because he knew what was going on already. When we rounded the corner, Eazy saw us coming down because of the way his cell was facing and immediately hopped up and tried to walk out of his cell, but Dez stopped him and pushed him back inside. I walked up right behind Dez and waited until Dez gave me the head nod, signaling I was in the clear to handle my business.

"Day two, Eazy, what's up, my nigga?" I said, not even going into the details because he knew what I was here for.

"Nigga my people dropped that shit off, and if they didn't, I don't know what to tell you," Eazy said, acting as if him not paying me was nothing to him.

"Nigga, you got one minute to tell me something or give up everything you got in the muthafucka," I told him. Yeah, he was definitely trying to pull my card and see what I was about, and he was going to find out.

"Man, like I said, you gotta wait until they pay shorty because you definitely not gettin' none of my commissary, nigga. Now get the fuck out my room," Eazy said as he thought I was just going to walk out and say okay. I walked towards the door and made sure there were no guards coming even though Dez was right there. I walked back in towards Eazy and punched him so hard in the mouth he flew backwards and onto the bed. He put his hands to his face and made sure his jaw wasn't broke and hopped back up, but it was too late. I pounced on him serving him left and right hits to the head and stomach. Eazy was able to get his feet to his chest and used all his strength he had in his legs and pushed me off of him with his feet. I fell backwards and hit my back on the toilet and felt a sharp pain shoot through my back, but I wasn't going to let that stop me. I got up off the floor just as he got off the bed, and we met in the middle of the tiny cell. Eazy now had blood running down his nose and a lump on the left side of his head, but that wasn't enough for him. He tried to rush me, but I was too quick and moved out the way, he ran right into the wall. I turned his way kicked him with the tip of my shoe, and he grunted in pain. I went in his cabinet that he kept his snacks in and grabbed everything I could conceal.

"Now, tell yo peoples next time it's going to be much worse," I said as I looked both ways before I walked out his cell and went straight to mine with Dez right on my heels. When we made it to my cell, I tossed Dez a couple packs of noodles that I grabbed from Eazy's cell, and he walked out my cell. I put the rest of my new snacks in my pile that I had accumulated and walked back out to GP. Eazy had cleaned his face up and was sitting with another one of the niggas that didn't like me, Mac. We all exchanged looks, and I laughed to myself. The nigga was Tuff Tony before he got that ass tagged, and now all of a sudden, he hiding behind another nigga that would get his ass beat if needed as well. I walked to the spades table and sat down and waited until they got done with the hand they were playing and told them I had next.

The whole day was like I was watching over my back because niggas didn't fight fair in jail, so I had to be on my toes at all times. Even when it was chow time, I sat in the corner with my back facing the walls so none of these niggas would think they were catching me slipping. That's what happened when you had to prove niggas couldn't play with you.

That night I finally got to see Sasha as she was making her rounds for the night, and I must admit that she was the most beautiful lady I had ever seen. I didn't know if it was because I was locked down and fantasized about her quite often or if she was really the prettiest female I had crossed paths with. When we spoke on the phone I couldn't call her by her name in fear of the operator catching on to our illegal business, so she instructed me to call her Mookie like her mother use too. I first I thought that shit was mad corny but I noticed how much she giggled when I called her that so it stuck with me and her. I couldn't wait until I was actually able to hold her and rub on her fat ass booty and just vibe. She has been showing me that she was down for a nigga and that she was a hustler at heart because she was handling my money for me, well at least that's what she was saying she was doing but of course I wouldn't know until I actually touched freedom. I always thought about what if she wasn't holding me down like I thought and actually fuck ing with my money, how I would handle things and honestly I didn't know. If anything I would probably write that off as a lost cause and kept it moving. I wasn't going to catch a domestic for some shit I shouldn't have been doing so fuck it. I wrote my lil baby another letter and folded up small enough to fit through our swapping spot and waited until she got to my cell door. I had to sit and listen to these bum ass niggas shoot their shot and make cat calls to her, being all types of disrespectful towards her and as bad as I wanted to let them niggas know what it was I couldn't because we had to keep shit on the down low. I told her once I'm out and back in a predicament to where I can fully provide for her like she needed to be she had to quit this job because I wasn't going. I don't see how her sucker ass ex boyfriend let her take this dangerous job when he was out there slanging work she would tell me. These niggas had it all backwards and I just didn't understand it because aint no way in hell my bitch would be working as a corrections officer, especially in the mens ward. When I heard her keys jiggling I walked to my door and leaned against the door frame, they had yet to lock the doors so I waited patiently.

"Inmate you need to take that sheet down from hanging over the bed like that" I heard her yell to one of the inmates. I knew why he hung the sheet over the bottom bunk like that, it was because them niggas was in the fucking and didn't want to get caught so they tried to create some privacy which they knew weren't going to work.

"Come on girl, let us get five minutes" One of the openly gay inmates said. He went by the name Cece. Even though all the inmates knew she was a man they didn't care. He carried himself like a women, dressed like a woman even went as far as sounding like a female, the only thing that kept him in the men's ward was the fact she was built like a sumo wrestler and had hands like Floyd Mayweather. You knew not to fuck with him because he had made plenty of examples out of niggas who thought he was a bitch and one thing you didn't want to do was get your bitch card pulled by a gay dude in jail. Sasha walked up to my cell and I was waiting on her with a big ass smile on my face per the usual. I didn't want to toot my own horn or any-thing but I knew I was fine ass nigga and I knew I had a million dollar smile that could finesse bitch out her drawls.

"There she goes" I said as I knew I had a couple seconds to talk with her.

"Inmate what you trying to conceal under the blanket" Sasha said as she entered my cell, acting as if she was looking for something. I looked out the door and made sure the coast was clear before I made the first move. I pulled her into me from the back, kissed her on the back of the neck and while her ass rubbed against the crotch of my pants. I spent her around and kissed her so deep I'm sure it made her panties wet. I didn't want to get carried away so I released her out my grip and she quickly walked back out the cell like nothing happen.

"Don't put the blanket over the window anymore or I am

going to have to write you up inmate" Sasha said trying to cover her tracks. That was my first time actually touching her let alone kissing her. I don't know what overcame me but I had to do it. I wanted her to have something to look forward to when I wasn't around and I knew that would be something she wouldn't forget. I started to get butterflies as I reminisced about our first kiss. Her lips were so soft and I could taste the thick strawberry flavored lip gloss that she had on. The way her ass was pushed up against my dick made me damn near bust in my pants. I knew I would be beating off to what just transpired when the cell doors closed tonight. I remembered when we were talking a while ago she said her favorite perfume was Chanel number five and I'm assuming that's what she had on because she smelled immaculate. Sasha smacked her own ass and walked out my cell and I couldn't help but laugh. She had a great personality and a funny sense of humor. I walked back out my cell and to the railing and looked over the edge, most inmates where now in their cell so the main floor was empty.

I couldn't help but stare at her while she made the rest of her rounds and went back downstairs. Every now and then she would turn to see if I was still looking at her and of course I was. I know she couldn't respond to me how she wanted to but the fact that she kissed me back was all I needed. They made the last sounding call telling us doors was about to close and I walked back in my cell where her perfume still lingered, and hopped on my top bunk. I was instantly horny so as soon as those doors closed, I pulled my boxers all the way off and started going to town on this dick with my right hand. The fact I could still taste her lipgloss on my lips made the process even more smooth. I envisioned myself bending Sasha over the leather couch she said she had in her living room and slowly inserted my thick long and cured nine inch dick in her awaiting wet and tight pussy canal. I saw myself stroking her slowly as i cupped and spread her ass cheeks. I gripped my dick a little harder, applying more pressure at the tip and stroked myself long and hard as I continued fantasizing.

Sasha pussy juices were dripping down her leg as I dug deep in her guts, trying to feel her cervix with the head of my dick and held it in place as she grinded all that ass on my pelvic bone. I imagined how her moans would sound while I sped the process up. I knew she liked her pussy played with while taking the dick from the back and how that made her kitty extra moist with her love juice. I closed my eyes as I felt my nut start to climb its way to the tip of my now throbbing dick. I couldn't stop my hips from thrusting into my hand as I still envisioned myself fucking the shit out of Sasha. I let my fantasy consume my thoughts as my stomach started to get more tight and my toes started to curl as I stroked my dick faster, making the grip more tightly.

"Hmmm" I moaned to myself as I propped myself up on my left elbow and let euphoria take over my entire body. When Sasha started throwing that ass back on me in my fantasy was when I lost it.

"Fuuckkkkk" I said in a low baritone as the nut came up my testicles and shot out my dick. I held a tight fist around my dick as my kids left the nest and squirted all over my covers. I convulsed vigorously and laid my head back down and against my pillow. My heart was racing as I panted like a dog out in a hundred degree. I laughed to myself as I caught my breath. That was the most enticing nut I had ever busted since I been locked down. I climbed off my bunk and damn near fell when I stood up on the floor as that nut made me weak to my knees. I walked a couple feet to the sink and washed myself up and hopped back in bed. My mind instantly drifted back to Sasha and I started daydreaming about what it would be like to have a future with her.

I must have fallen asleep after a long night with myself because I'm normally up before the sun comes up but today I guess I slept later than usual. I woke up to my cell door being open and Mickey looking directly at me. I felt vulnerable at the instant because I didn't know exactly how long he had been standing there.

"Damn nigga what the fuck you want" I said as I noticed he had yet to say anything but had a creepy smirk on his face.

"Get up inmate and pack your shit, you outta here" He said smiling. I was confused because I didn't have a cellmate and I didn't want to switch cells.

"Why the fuck they switching my cell Mickey" I asked him as I sat up and wiped the sleep out of my eyes. I knew he would let me know what was going on.

"You not switching cells buddy, you getting released" Mickey said cheesing. Now I was definitely confused because I hadn't gotten any mail saying my appeal was granted or even that I was getting released.

"Yea fucking right stop bullshitting me" I said now getting mad because I didn't play like this.

"Get yo shit and lets go. You out this bitch. Go ask them questions to processing" He said as he waited for me to get up.

"I know you fucking lying" I said to myself and got out the bed so quick when I got on my feet it felt like they were still sleep. I didn't care as I hurried and threw all my shit in an empty pillow case and walked out my cell. I glanced at the clock and it was six in the morning and everyone else was still locked down. I was shocked and confused at what was happening because I didn't think I would be getting out any time soon but low and behold there I was. Mickey escorted me straight to processing to start my process out of here. When I was granted my one phone call I called my cousin Bud. That was the only nigga that actually made sure I was straight and kept the communication open between us. Bud and I did a lot of dirt back in the day and he was the one that got me knee deep into the drug game so me calling him was a must.

"What's up cousin" I asked him as soon as the operator was done talking.

"Shit making money. What's the word lil cuz" He asked me.

"They bout to release a nigga" I said with much enthusiam.

"Yea fucking right" he said sounding as confused like me.

"How nigga" He asked and I didn't know want to tell him my truth a so I told him I didnt know. We talked for a couple minutes and I had him call Sasha on three way. I knew she wasn't yet at work so I hoped that she answered a number she didn't know and luckily she did.

"Hello" Sasha answered sounding like I had just woke her up.

"Rise and Shine my Mookie" I said sounding happy.

"Hey boo. Who you have calling me and why you calling so early" She asked.

"What's your address. I don't have that much time left" I asked her. She gave me her address and kept asking why I needed it and how was I able to call her so early. She knew my schedule so I knew she knew something wasn't right.

"Its lit! They releasing me" I said sounding more excited than I ever had.

"Yea fucking right Carlos dont play with me" Sasha said now sounding like she was more alert and fully woke out of her sleep.

"I'm in processing now. They said about another couple hours and Ima be walking out this bitch" I could tell Sasha was now up moving around.

"I'm bout to schedule a lyft for a couple hours!" She said sounding like she was panicking almost.

"What the fuck is a lyft Mookie" I asked her.

"A cab nigga" she said laughing. I was serious as hell though. I finished up the conversation and told Bud I would call him as soon as I got to my destination. They let me call my case worker as a courtesy call so I made that phone call and he picked up right away. He went on to explain to me that they reviewed my case and seen I had nothing to do with the incident in the cafe and being that I cooperated during trial, I was being released.. I didn't ask no other questions but was told that I needed to show up for weekly meetings with my P.O. After about an hour of paperwork and going over my some legal aspects, I was walking up out that jam a free man!

Chapter 15

Sasha

When I got off the phone with Los, my heart started to race. I couldn't believe they released him all of a sudden, and I didn't know how to feel. I was overwhelmed with emotion and started hyperventilating almost. Carlos and I talked about this moment a lot, and after sharing our first random yet quick kiss, to him being released had me feeling like the happiest women alive. I looked around my apartment and noticed it was a bit junky and could use some straightening up so I went to the playlist on my phone and started my music and connected the bluetooth. As I bobbed my head to Kalid's *Can We Just Talk* and put my phone on the dresser as I grew excited. My baby will be here in a couple hours. I fantasized about how it would feel to actually be in his arms and I was about to get that chance. I also remembered that I hadn't went grocery shopping yet either and I knew he would want a home cooked meal for when he gets here. I hopped on my computer and did online grocery shopping at Walmart and set the delivery for a couple hours because I didn't feel like going outside.

"Fuck!" I said as I remembered that I had to work the second shift today and that killed my mood instantly. I was definitely not about to miss the first moment with my man. I had been full time for months now so I figured I had PTO that I could use so I took advantage of it. I grabbed my phone and practiced my 'sick' talk so I would make it actually believable and took the chance. I dialed my managers number and put on the best act I have ever done and surprised my damn self when he believed me and didn't question it.

RISKING IT ALL FOR A CONVICT

Suckassss

I laughed to myself as I continued to clean up. Carlos said he would be released in about an hour and that was about thirty minutes ago. I knew it would take longer than that because I have been trained on booking out paperwork and it takes a couple hours, yet I still ordered the Lyft for a couple hours out so push comes to shove, he would have to wait until it came. As I was cleaning I stopped and lit some of my candles that I bought from Victoria Secrets and that gave me the idea to put on one of my sexy lingerie outfits that were collecting dust in the back of my closet and I already know which one I would put on. I wasn't skinny by far but I was thick with a slim waist and I know that baby gone have a field day with all this ass. I noted to myself that I needed to grab a plan b tomorrow before work because I had a thought on how tonight was going to go and how it was going to end.

It took me about forty five minutes to get my house the way I wanted and by the time I was done I got a notification that my groceries were on the way to being delivered. Los had told me a while back that his favorite meal was a surf and turf consisting of steak, shrimp and a butter sauce, a loaded baked potato and broccoli on the side. Luckily for him, I was a beast at this cooking shit so he was about to get one of the best meals he had ever had. The candles aroma started making its way throughout the house and I had opened all my windows and doors since it was late september so it was a cool breeze coming through. I glanced at the clock and it said it was almost noon and I had last talked with Carlos at about ten so I'm sure he would be showing up soon. While I started making my man his dinner I opened my wine that I had in the fridge and poured me a big cup full. I loved me some moscato and had a full stock of it under my cabinet and a couple of them in my fridge. Dinner took about an hour to complete and surprisingly he wasn't there yet so I had time to take me a quick bath and get dolled up.

My phone rang and I noticed it was the number that he had called me from. Bud was his cousin that he always spoke about. He went on to tell me that he was officially released and was on his way to me. He had said that he missed the cab I sent him so he ordered another one for him. It didn't take that long to get to my house from Minneapolis so I gulped down my wine and ran to the bathroom and hoped in the shower. I made sure I used the good body wash and made sure I washed every nook and cranny to the T. My stomach started fluttering as I thought about the moment that was about to happen. I washed up and got out the shower without a towel to be able to air dry while I looked for the sexy teddy lingerie that I was thinking about wearing. Even though I wasn't self conscious I was still nervous about seeing him and me putting someting sexy on for the first time of us actually seeing each other made me feel a bit insecure But fuck it. I grabbed the bag that was all the way in the back of the closet and grabbed the blue teddy set that still had the tags attached and slipped it on my now dry skin. I oiled my body down in lavender oil and sprayed on my Ralph Lauren Romance perfume I bought for myself a while back. I was rocking my natural hair in a wrap until I got paid next so I could get my hair done, so I ununwrapped my hair and let it fall over my shoulders and plugged in my flat irons so I can feather it out a little but, even though I know I'm going to sweat it out later. I applied some simple eye liner and Mascara and some Mac lip gloss and was ready to officially meet the man I've been waiting for. I looked on the dresser and noticed I never finished smoking my blunt so I grabbed the lighter and lit it. I was already feeling the one cup of wine that I had downed and I knew this blunt was gone sit right. I turned my music back on off my phone and connected it to the speaker. Walking around my room looking fine as hell, I started to get a little sache in my walk. For some reason *Movies* by Ashanti was playing in my head so I played it on youtube and put it on repeat. That was my jam from back in the day and is still my jam today. I walked in front of my dresser and looked in the mirror and started rolling my hips. I was feeling myself so to me I was the next Shakira.

Knock knock

I could have heard those faint knocks in the middle of a football game. I grew nervous and started fanning my face like I was in ninety degree weather.

"Okay bitch. Yo man is here. Stop acting scary" I said to myself as I heard him knock again. I walked to the front door and looked through the peephole. I saw Carlos standing there in a white t-shirt, some blue shorts and some crispy white forces. I assumed this was what he was wearing when he got locked up. He had a white durag wrapped around his head and a diamond earring in his left ear. His left hand rested on my door and his right hand held a brown paper bag. Carlos had his head tilted sideways like he was tired of waiting for me to open the door. I couldn't help but admire how fine he was and the fact that I never noticed that he was bowlegged. I started unlocking the door while still looking out the peep hole and saw a smile spread across his face.

Jesus this man, my man, was fine as fuck!

I opened the door and struck a pose as I tried my best to look my sexiest. When we laid eyes on each other, it was like a magical moment that I never wanted to forget. It was a beautiful silence as we admired each other with our eyes. He looked me up and down and started biting his lips and I couldn't take it anymore. I stepped back seductively, allowing him to enter into my home and did a 360 turn, making sure to stop when my ass was facing him so he could get a perfect view. I turned back towards him and he was just cheesing hard and it made me giggle. Carlos threw his brown paper bag on the couch and removed his shoes and placed them neatly by the door. He faced me and started walking towards me and I met him halfway.

"Finally, we officially meet" I said with a big grin on my face. I wrapped my hands around his neck and inhaled his scent deeply.

"Finally my Mookie in my arms" Carlos said as he wrapped his arms tightly around my waist and caressed my back with his large and smooth hand. His hands crept slowly down my back and palmed my ass. He let out a slight moan and that made me push my body harder against his, my titties now pressed against his chest. It was like at that moment nothing else matters and our spirits intertwined in one. I felt like at this moment, anything before this didn't matter and anything after would just be a blessing. Carlos and I danced around the living room to no music and just enjoyed each other's presence for the time being. After a couple minutes of silence and love, he pulled away from me and looked me in my eyes and gave me the best kiss I have ever received in my life.

"Something smells good mama" He said as he looked to the side of me to the kitchen.

"I know you said your favorite meal was a surf and turf, so that's what I got made for you baby" I said as I pulled his hand and led him to the kitchen.

"All this ass Sash" Los said as he pulled me back and let my ass rub against his crotch.

"I thought you were hungry" I said turning around and embracing him again while walking backwards into the kitchen.

"I am. Ima eat this steak and shrimp than devour you for dessert" Carlos said whispering in my ear, making my panties soak and wet.

"I know you are. Is it coo I smoke around you or is that a no no?" I asked him in a serious tone.

"Na, you good my Mookie. Smoke yo shit. Hell I can't wait to get to smoke me a blunt. I got thirty days" Carlos replied. I had everything in the oven warming so I wouldn't have to heat it up in the microwave. I made Los his plate and a tall glass of his favorite strawberry kool aid and brought it in bedroom and turned on the cable. I don't know why but I wanted to make him feel like he was being catered to by a real woman and I think I was doing the damn thang! I was being cautious and decided that I wasn't going to smoke around him until he was for sure off papers so I told him that I would smoke in the living room while he ate his food in the room.

I grabbed my fleece throw blanket off chair I had in the corner of my room and walked in the living room and turned on my sixty inch TV. Fresh Prince was on BET so I sat and smoked while watching one of my favorite episodes, the one when they had an earthquake and Will Smith got stuck in the basement. I must have been laughing loudly because it made Los come in the living room to see what was so funny and by then I was already high, my eyes red and low.

"Damn, this what you look like when you smoke, all chinky eyed and shit. Okay sexy" Los said as he sat by my side. I put my blunt out as he stretched his legs and out in front of him and put his arm around me. I cuddled up next to him and started running my fingers through his beard.

"Thank you Sasha" Carlos said as he intertwined his fingers with mines and lifted my hand to his mouth and kissed the back of my hand.

"For what baby" I asked, looking confused.

"Being here for a nigga. Holding shit down and jeopardizing your job for me. I don't know how to thank you enough. You a real one Mookie" He said to me while gazing in my eyes. I didn't know what to say and he knew that so instead of waiting for my response, he pulled me on top of him and pulled my head down for another kiss. I kissed him passionately as I straddled his lap. Carlos rubbed both my ass cheeks as I grinded my pelvic bone against his. He unclasped my bra and my size forty four double d breast were staring him directly in his face. I heard Carlos breath in and grunted as he let go of my ass and grabbed my breast and let his tongue circle my areola as I started to feel a bulge in between my legs. I reached down to start undoing his pants when he lightly pulled me off of him so he could stand up. I sat back on the couch as I watched him pull his shirt from over his head and I damn near melted in my skin. Carlos had a body of a god! He had tattoos covering his whole torso and even though he didn't have a abs his buff and stacked chest and his muscular shoulders made up for it. Carlos didn't have a belly either but you could see that he continuously worked out. My baby was just fine as hell.

Carlos than dropped his pants that he had on and grabbed his dick through his boxers and I took that as my cue. I sat on the end of the couch as he stood directly in front of me. I looked up at him from below and pulled his boxers down to his ankles and he stepped out of them. I knew Carlos was packing but damn he was carrying a third leg in between his thighs. He looked down at me and started laughing because he knew what I was thinking. I grabbed his dick with both my hands and sucked on the tip lightly and worked my way down the shaft until I hit rock bottom. I used my mouth as a vacuum cleaner and started sucking his dick like there was no tomorrow. I used my hands to jerk him off at the same time that my mouth was slurping him up. Carlos instantly started squirming and pushed my head off of him.

"Girl you must have forgot I just got out. If you want this dick you can't be giving me this award winning scholar head, you know how quick I just almost busted" He said pulling me up by neck softly and kissing me deep.

"Well let me help you bust this first nut so I can help you bust the second one" I whispered to him as he turned me around and bent me over the arm of the couch. He slid my thong to the side and spread my ass checks and rubbed his dick up and down my pussy until he slowly stuck his dick in my awaiting love box. It was like his dick was made for my kitty because even though it hurt a bit as he stuck it in, being that I havent had no dick since

Anthony, and he had way more hang time than that nigga, it was a little painful, but once he got fully in it, my walls relaxed and allowed him to pursue his happiness inside of me.

"Fuck" I heard him whisper. I looked back and Los had his eyes closed as he was biting his juicy bottom lip. That made my world spin and made me go even harder. I pushed him back so I could have more room on the couch. I then proceeded to lay on my stomach than tooted my ass up in the air and made my back arch low.

"Damn" Los said as he got in between my legs and glided his dick from the front of my pussy to the back teasing my orgasm. I reached down under me and grabbed his dick and put it in myself. He was playing and I couldn't take it. Carlos laughed at my aggressiveness and started hitting all my spots that I didn't know I had. Me arching my back until I couldn't arch it anymore gave him all the access he needed for a full examination of my cervix with his dick. I couldn't hinder the great sensational ecstasy that my body was going through. I cried to God himself as Carlos cranked up his speed, everytime his pelvic hit my ass the vibration of my ass jiggling also aided in the best orgasm that I was ever going to have in my life.

"I'm about to cum baby. Fuck! I moaned as I felt my whole body go weak.

"Don't tap out baby. Give me a couple more seconds" Los said as i felt his strokes quicken.

Aw shit! Fuckkk" Los moaned in pure bliss. Carlos leaned over my limp body as his soul left his body. He fell backwards on the couch and I sat up, hair disheveled all over my head. Los was sweating bullets and trying to catch his breath as I watched his chest heaved up and down.

"Welcome home daddy" I said as I stood up and pulled him to his feet. I led him by hand to the bedroom that we would now share and planned to get that second nut up out of him.

Chapter 16

Anthony

Riding around with Angel handling business was the move for the day, and it was always a pleasure. My lil' baby was a go getta, and that's why I fucked with her. I met Angel a couple months ago when I had pulled up to a party that she was at, selling some of her people some weed. This was when me and Sasha officially cut all ties with each other, and I became a little thot. Yeah, I could admit when she actually told me she didn't want to be with me and meant it, a nigga was heartbroken. They say you don't know what you missin' until it's gone, and I felt that shit. I fucked up, and after the umpteenth time of trying to talk to her and she wanted nothing to do with me, I gave up and moved on.

As far as Brittani was concerned, I still kept in contact with her every now and then because she hadn't stop calling me since I came and stayed with Angel. Brittani was extremely clingy, and I instantly regretted even entertaining her ass, though she was the one who came on to me first. I still remember that day like it was yesterday.

It was a day when Sasha was at work, and I had seen Brittani at the corner store ,and she said she had left her ID at our house and really needed it for something, and that Sasha knew she was going to stop by. I didn't think nothing of it because it wouldn't had been the first time she popped up unannounced and Sasha didn't say anything. We rode in our separate cars and parked in the back driveway like Sasha and I normally parked and she followed me to the door. When I put the key in the lock

I felt Brittani's hand wrap around me and rub up and down my stomach through my shirt and I froze up. This was the first time she tried anything like this but by the way she sometimes looks at me, gave me an idea that she was feeling me. I gently pushed her hand away and looked around to make sure no one seen her and opened the door and she pushed me in. As soon as we were in the house I closed the door and Brittani pounced on me like prey in the wild. She started kissing all on me and a couple seconds later she was pulling my pants down and putting my dick in her mouth and the rest is all she wrote and like a dummy, I didnt stop her either.

Angel was the real deal though. Her and Sasha was like night and day and Angel was my night for sure. She was more up-beat and courageous while Sasha was more laid back type. Sasha was a homebody, even though there was nothing necessarily wrong with that, that shit gets boring and that's when the accusations starts because I don't want to sit in the house around her ass all day. They were complete opposites and I can honestly admit that Angel was more up my alley.

Even though I wasn't the man of my city I was planning to make a name for myself in the streets. Angel came from a long line of drug dealers and hustlers so when she came into my life she tighten my ass up and showed me some things about the game I had to admit I didn't know and in turn it got my paper flowing in like never before. I wasn't serving much in the city because they already had to many niggas tryna sell to the same clients and they didn't like that, that's how war starts. So I decided to get in tune with the country folks, the big dollas, the white people. I went from serving Pooky down the block to serving Billy, the vice president of a law firm. That's where all the money was and you know word of mouth is a muthafucka so when they got in tune with me, they put their friends, co workers, grandmas, everybody on!

Angel and I waere out looking at this building that was for

sale because I was about to open a barbershop in the hood and I couldn't wait. This had been one of my plans for 2019 and I'm glad I had the courage to do it. Baby helped me find the build my credit up to where it needed to be, she helped me put the money up and overall helped me with the entire process and for that I would forever be grateful for her. Of course she had a ten percent of the deal because she was a big help in the process. The new shop would be located on Dale St, right in the hood. I specifically wanted it in this neighborhood because not only is that where I grew up at, but thats where a lot of niggas be at. I just don't want to open a barbershop I wanted to be able to reach out to the boys with no guidance, for them to be able to have a safe place and not have to worry about if they would get to eat that day, or if they need help with homework or some shit. I guess being with someone who will change you mentally is the person you need in your life, only if your willing to change yourself and that's what I find with Angel.

"So, you liked the building, papi?" she asked me as we drove the short distance to Hickory Hut, a local chicken joint down the street. Their chicken use to hit and I havent had any in awhile so I decided to stop there for lunch.

"Yea, I like it and it's in a nice location. I can't wait to open up shop and get the ball rolling." I told her as I pulled into the parking lot and let Angel run in and grab our food that we pre ordered already. I saw a lot of little niggas sitting outside the restaurant and that reminded me of myself before I made myself a name. It was like four of them trying to get high off of one blunt so I decided to pay it forward.

"Aye. Aye young nigga" I called out and waited to see which one of them were going to turn around and answer me. Surprisingly it was the one that wasn't engaged in the loud conversation his friends were having and actually noticed that I was talking to them, stood up and looked at me. I nodded for him to come here and he walked over, looking around, being aware of his surroundings.

"Wassup, bro?" he said as he stood a couple feet from my window. I started to take a liking to this lil' nigga already.

"Why y'all posted at these people's establishment like that, smoking and shit?" I asked him.

"Aye Leeky, who you talking to bru?" one of his boys asked him from across the parking lot. He just looked at him and didn't say nothing.

"It's early, and I'm waiting on my bus to head to this bull-shit ass job. What you need old head?" He asked me as I saw his eyes wander over me, looking at my freshness and my jewelry.

"I saw you and your boys smoking on one blunt, so I was gon' throw y'all a sack. I know times hard out here, so I decided to be nice," I said as I took a sack out of my hidden compartment in my door and handed it to him. Instead of bringing it to his boys, he put it in his pocket and made sure they didn't see him.

"Oh, you not sharing with yo man over there?" I asked him.

"Na, fuck them niggas. I wasn't smoking that wack shit they smoking, and they should have came over here to see what you wanted and being that they didn't, it wasn't meant for them to have it" He laughed. It was something about this kid that I couldn't put my finger on but I felt a wave a good energy coming from him.

"Damn baby you fine as hell" I heard one of his boys say to Angel as she walked out of the store.

"Girl you know what I could do with all that ass" Another one yelled to her as she walked back to the car with our bags of food.

"Ayo, chill the fuck out. Dont you see her nigga sitting right here dude." The kid at my window yelled to his disrespectful ass friends. I didn't say anything to the teenagers because I knew I had a loyal bitch and them lil niggas couldn't touch her with a ten foot pole, also because I was too old to be arguing with them. I was surprised that homie standing here said something, that showed me a sign of respect.

"What's your name lil homie?" I asked him.

"Mailk, my niggas call me Leeky though" he said.

"You sold weed before Leeky" I asked him blunty.

"A little here and there.. I thought about it but these niggas product is wack and im not about to waste my time with it." He said as he put his hand in his pocket and grabbed his phone. He checked the time and noticed he was about to miss his bus.

"Aye gotta go. My bus about to come." He said looking at me, seeing if I wanted anything else from him. I took my business card out and handed it to him.

"You seem like a solid nigga. Hit me up if you want to make some real money homie. Only you, Dont pass my number around to them niggas B" I said as I started my car. He looked at the card for a second then stuck it in his pocket.

"Ima holla at you when I get off."

"Bet." I said and put my car in reverse and maneuvered out their small ass parking lot.

"You recruiting now baby" Angel asked me.

"Something like that." I told her. I'm trying to build my team up so if I recognize something in someone ima speak on it."

"I feel you papi."

It was about ten in the morning and I was done with my errands for the time being and I was just ready to lay up with my bitch and let my money make itself. I had my dutch blunts and my weed and a fat ass to rub on so it was going to be a chilled Saturday. When we finally made it home the sweet smell of those expensive ass aromatherapy candles filled my nostrils. Angels candle choice today was mandarin berry scented and that shit smelled amazing. Baby laid our food out for us and rolled my blunt for me as I changed out of my business clothes and into my basketball shorts and went back into the living room to chill and eat. We turned on lifetime and started to watch some crazy ass movie about a deranged babysitter and smoked. My phone started to vibrate and I looked down to see that it was Brittani. This girl called numerous times a day to the point where I didn't have a choice but to tell Angel who she was because if I didn't, she would have started to assume shit and I didn't need that. I didn't tell her that I still fucked her from time to time just the situation that lead up to her damn near stalking me. Brittani was in her feelings because I wasn't giving her the time that she wanted and I didn't plan too. I wouldn't dare wife a bitch that was fucking her friend nigga and she didn't get that.

"Why is she calling again?" Angel asked me.

'Iono shit. I haven't talked to this bitch in a minute, since the last time I told her to stop calling." I lied. I spoke with her last week after I let her suck my dick at her crib but I told her she had to let up on all this calling me and shit. As long as she allowed me to keep some of my work and money stashed in her crib, I had to keep her on a loose string.

"Mhhmm" Angel replied to me as she snuggled closer to me and we finished our netflix and chill session. I knew she didn't trust me but I also knew she was rocking with me so I tried to keep my bullshit at a minimum. There was a knock on the door and I stood up confused because I wasn't expecting anyone. I looked out the peephole and seen Fab standing there. I opened the door and walked back to the living room while Fab came in and shut the door, following behind me.

"Wassup Angel" He greeted her as she grabbed a couple more pieces of chicken, the blunt that we eventually put out and walked out of the living room.

'Hey Fab. Estaré' arriba si me necesitas papi." Angel said,

telling me she would be upstairs if I needed her.

"Okay mamacita" I said to her as I heard the door close upstairs.

"Man why she ain't hooked me up with one of her sisters or something. I want me a spanish bitch too nigga" Fab said as he took his shoes off and propped his feet up on Anthonys ottoman.

"Shit ask her when she come back down here nigga. What yo ass want this early" I asked him throwing him the controller to my game system.

"Shit. I just left Niecy crib and I don't feel like dealing with my BM and why I didn't come in last night." Fab said as he lit the blunt he took from behind his ear and lit it. I just shook my head and finished setting up the game. We played online COD for about an hour, talking shit before I brought up business shit.

"I found a spot for the barbershop" I told him as we kept our eyes on the T.V.

"Word. Which building?" he asked me.

"The one of dale. Fuck!" I said as I answered him and got killed at the same time.

"The one we rode past by the gas station"

"Yep. I think we bout to seal the deal. That muthafucka nice and a good price" I said. It got quiet and I knew what was to come next.

"So, have you thought about it?" he asked me refering to if I was going to let him run the shop and like before, I didn't know what I was going to do. Fab was my nigga and all but as far as letting him run my business, with no type of experience with running a business at all, he didn't have a barbers license either, I doubt I would let him but for now I was going to keep going with the flow.

"Na ghee, I haven't thought about what I was going to do yet. When it gets close to opening, I'll make my decision. Nigga, have you even looked into taking some of those business course and shit like we talked about a couple weeks ago? I told you I'm not going to just throw you in there without no knowledge of how a business is supposed to be ran." I said honestly and just like I thought, he hadn't.

"Na, but ima get on it nigga damn" Fab said like I was irritating him with it or something.

" Good" I said as we continued on with our game. It was a typical Saturday so I planned to hang around the house all day.

"Aye Buddy supposed to slide through he said. I told him I was on my way over here and he said he had something to talk to you about anyway." Fab said. Buddy was a nigga I occasionally did business with. He was a cool as nigga from Chicago and he was trying to eat like the rest of us, that was my nigga even though we rarely kicked it like that.

"Cool. Text that nigga and see where he at because I need some more woods anyway" I told him.

"I dont know how you gone take this but word around town was that Sasha got a new nigga" Fab said as he kept playing the game. That shit took me back at first and then started to make me mad for some reason.

"And you just now telling me nigga?" I asked him as my heart rate started to speed up.

"Yea the fuck. You got a whole bitch so I didn't think you gave a fuck, shit I aint heard you bring her name up in months." Fab said as I paused the game and looked at him.

"What nigga" he asked me with a confused look on his face.

"What new nigga" I repeated myself before I gave him a chance to answer. I put my controller down and walked to the bottom of my steps, making sure my bedroom door was closed.

I didn't want Angel to hear shit.

"Nigga I dont know. I aint seen her with nobody but some of the boys out in the hood was asking me was she up for grabs now cuz they seen here with this buff nigga a couple times." Fab told me.

"Na, i aint heard about no new nigga, but I heard she moved out the old place and got her a new crib anyway so whatever" I brushed it off like I didn't care but deep down inside a nigga feelings were hurt. Yea I know I shouldn't give a fuck but fuck that. It hit different when you get to thinking another nigga treating you bitch the way she should have been treated by you. My stomach was in knots thinking about somebody else making her happy.

Fab looked at me, shook his head and laughed. That nigga knew me like a can of paint so he knew I was hurt and he knew I didn't want to talk about it. I knew this day was going to come eventually so I been mentally prepared myself for this wave of emotions that I knew were to come. We continued to play the game until I heard another knock at the door. Fab got up and opened it and I heard him and Buddy greeting each other at the door. Buddy walked in the living room first and dapped me up before taking a seat in my chair he knew I didn't like no one sitting in. I looked at him like he was crazy and he started laughing.

"Damn nigga you still tight in the ass about this damn recliner." He said as he got up and sat next to Fab on the love seat.

"Clearly. What's up my brother" I responded.

"Shit. Getting to this money like usual." See, Buddy, as we call him was this lowkey quiet nigga from the suburbs that got money and went on about his business. He was the one that got me the white collar folks. Buddy wanted nothing to do with the white work I was pushing and he had his own hustle going on so we just made sure to keep connected with each other so we

RISKING IT ALL FOR A CONVICT

could know whats going on in each others neck of the woods.

"I see. I see that new ice on your wrist my dude" I said referring to the new iced out rolex Buddy was sporting. See me, I wasn't that big on jewelry, maybe a chain or pinky ring here or there but nothing too extravagant. Buddy pulled out the pack of backwoods I asked him to grab for me from the store and asked can he use one to roll up and of course I said yea. We sat, chilled and smoked for a couple hours before Angel came back downstairs and asked us were we hungry because she was about to make something to eat. We all agreed and she said she was going to make some loaded chicken fries that she made regularly.

"You know how I do brotha" Buddy smiled as he held up his wrist for them to get a clearer view.

"But check it out. My little cousin just got out the pen about a week ago, did two years and the nigga tryna get his feet wet and get some quick change in his pocket. You think you can front him some work?" Buddy asked me. I sat there before I answered him because I normally didn't fuck with dudes coming out the fed.

"Ima think on that and get back to you. You know how I feel about that" I told Buddy. The last time I fucked with a thirsty nigga just getting out the nigga took my work and bread and I hadn't heard from him sense, but that was a while ago and I still had my guards up for fuck shit like that.

"Ok. Well I just wanted to stop through and chop it up with yall before I head to my side of town. Ima hit you in a couple days and see what you say. He legit and if you decided to fuck with him I could bring em by and let you check him out" Buddy said as he stood up and dapped me and Fab before walking out the door. Hell I needed all the good runners I could get because these next couple moves I was planning to make required me to have a solid team that was hungry like I was.

Chapter 17

Los

It had been a week since I touched down, and a free man, and even though much hadn't changed, a lot had changed for me mentally. I had met with my PO, and he did give me the good news that after a couple more weeks I wouldn't be on papers anymore and I would officially be my own man again. At least having that to look forward too was good. I went out and job searches every day like baby wanted me too but of course with my background and me being freshly released out of jail no one was going to hire me, a felon. I knew what it was before I got re-leased so I had to prepare myself while I was incarcerated that I may had to get my feet wet one more time, but this time would be just until I got myself together than I would be done. I needed quick money and fast and me trying to get a good job was a far stretch. I had spoken with my cousin Bud a couple days ago and he said he had a simple job for me that would put a couple hundred in my pocket and he also told me he was going to talk to his mans to see if I could get put on for a minute. I didn't plan to not be legit it was just as a man, I just couldn't sit around while my girl went to work everyday, gave me money to get to where I needed to go and just overall taking care of me like I was her child. Nah, I couldn't do that shit. It made me feel like a whole bitch when she does for me even though she tells me a million times she just holding me down until I come up. I haven't told her about the run Bud wanted me to do because I didn't want her flipping out on me like I knew she would so I kept that little se-cret to myself.

The drop was tonight and Bud needed me to take the van

full of drugs to the other side of town and drop the van off at a location where someone would be waiting to pick it up. In my head it was simple because I wouldn't be touching nothing dirty and he assured me it would be a quick drive so I wouldn't be driving dirty that long. Of course the thought of me getting caught and sent back to jail crossed my mind numerous of times but I pushed it back and grew some balls. Jail would make a nigga either never want to do something that would land him back in the hell hole, or it would make his skin more thick and make him more of a menace. I had to tell myself like nigga, you was just selling drugs inside them walls so why grow cold feet now. I was never the type of dude that worked a regular nine to five anyway and that quick and easy money was just to appealing for me not to get. I had a lot of time until midnight, which is when I was going to make my run so I decided to do what has been on my mind the whole time I was locked up and that was to reach out to the nigga that was supposed to be my right hand man, the one that wasn't suppose to switch up on me like he did, Nas. That shit still got to me every time I thought about how he walked in the house that night and I haven't seen or heard from him since. From what I heard, Big Meechie was now locked up facing thirty years for all the damage he has done throughtout the city and at first I felt bad but as I started to think about it, fuck dude ass.

I was laying down on the bed watching Sasha as she was getting ready for work and I was in awe. I could never get tired of watching her. She was like an angel that was sent down from heaven, personally created for me. The way she been down for a nigga these past couple months has really shown me that she is a true thoroughbred female. We had just had yet another bomb ass sex session before she had to leave for work, and she had came into the bedroom from showering and had nothing on but a towel. My dick instantly grew solid so I laid on my back and watch as the sheet that I had covering my dick become a tent.

"You know your beautiful right" I asked her as she turned

143

my way and her eyes fell from my face to the hump in the sheets.

"Yes I do, you tell me all day everyday and no, I am not about to be late because you can't get enough of my loving." Sasha laughed as she walked to my side of the bed and planted a kiss so sweet on my lips. Sasha knew she wanted to feel me inside of her because she started rubbing my dick through the sheets and that was all she needed to do. I looked at the clock and noticed she had forty five minutes until she had to leave for work and all I needed was ten. I stood up and she tried to stand up to but I gently pushed her back onto the bed.

"Where you think you going" I said as I spread her legs and got on my knees.

"You wasn't gone feed yo manz before you left" I asked her as I started kissing in between her juicy thighs. I knew she had to go so I wasn't going to prolong it, I still wanted to feel her insides with my dick. I nestled my face in her pussy before I started my quick pleasure releaser. French kissing her pearl tongue, I grabbed both thighs and spread them apart a little further and she arched her back. I acted as if her clitoris and my tongue was slow dancing together. Sasha taste so damn good and her scent would give me goose bumps. It was like her pussy was just perfect.

"Aagh. Fuck baby keep it right there" Sasha moaned as she held my head in place, right at the opening of her sweetness. I stuck my tongue in her love box and made flickering motion, making sure the tip of my tongue hit the top of her canal, rubbing the spongy part that they considered the g spot and she instantly came. If she didn't have to work I would have kept going. Her orgasm was intense because her legs started shaking and her eyes wear rolling in the back of her head.

"Yesssss daddy. Om my god" She moaned as she rubbed my waves. I stood up and smiled as I licked my lips that held all her juices. She tried to get up and I let her, but when she was fully on her feet she kissed me, tasting her pussy and at that moment

I just wanted her to ride this dick but knew she couldn't. I spun her around and bent her over the edge of the bed.

"Bay no, I gotta gooooo-" I stuck my dick in her warm and tight pussy and that shut her up. She was already ready for me so it wouldn't take me long to bust a quick one. Sasha reached under her and started playing with her pussy as I spread her ass cheeks so I can dig into it deeper. I noticed that when she played with herself when I was hitting it, it made the kitty way more wet and also made her orgasms more intense.

"I'm coming again Carlos. Fuck baby keep going" Sasha muffled as she put her face in the now moisten sheets. I felt a gush of wetness invade her pussy therefor making my strokes feel like my dick was swimming in waves. I felt her pussy walls convulse and that sent me over the edge. I was fresh out so them nuts still came quick, whether I wanted them to or not. After about ten more deep strokes I was attaching my kids to her cervix.

"Fuckkkkkk" my knees became weak and I accidently fell onto her back. That nut for some reason felt like one of the best ones I've had since me and Sasha started having sex. This girl just did something to me.

Sasha pushed me off her back and ran to the bathroom to wash herself up. She definitely was going to be late, just a couple minutes late though but it was all worth it. I took my muscle shirt off and got in bed and closed my eyes as I listened to her rip and run throughout the crib making sure she had everything she needed for work, while cursing me out at the same time.

"I knew I shouldn't had started with yo ass. Now ima be fucking late Los damn" She said as she hopped around trying to put her cargo pants on.

"So you just gone go to sleep before I even walk out the door huh? I know this pussy good but damn boo you ain't even gone walk me to the door" I heard her say as she laughed. I opened one of my eyes and caught her looking at me like she was in love, and lowkey I was starting to feel it anyway.

"Boo do you see how that nut just weakened my ass. I can't get up if I wanted too. You just took my soul, and my heart" I said as I smiled at her. I told her I would get up and lock the top lock and for her to just lock the bottom, she kissed me goodbye and left out and just like that, I feel asleep like a kid that just got his ass whooped, damn this girl is the shit.

I slept for about two hours after Sasha left and I felt rejuvenated. I had to put some shit in motion and sitting on my ass all day wasn't going to help. I got up and took a hot shower and threw on a white tee and some basketball shorts Sasha got for me while I was locked up. I still had some money saved from when baby was bringing that work in for me so I wasn't completely on my ass. She had took me to the store and I had grabbed some all white forces because those go with everything and some cologne that she had grabbed for me and put it on. Sasha also made sure I had a phone to use while I was out so I grabbed that off the charger and sat back on the bed now fully dressed. I contemplated if I was going to call Nas because I just had to know if he was still rocking with me or not. He was the only one that I knew for sure knew that I snitched on Meechie so our bond was now questionable. I dialed the number that I knew by heart and lowkey hoped he changed it but once it started ringing I knew that he hadn't. I waited a couple seconds and he finally answered.

"Wassup who dis" Nas said into the phone over what seemed to be a baby crying.

"Los" His end of the phone went silent for a second.

"Stop fucking playing with me who the fuck is this" Nas asked agaiin not believing that I was out.

"Nasir, it's me nigga" I said using his government. He hated when I said his real name.

"You know I don't like doing three way calls Carlos. Whats good my guy" He asked nonchalantly, like he wasn't ignoring my jail calls for the past two years.

"Nigga I been out for about a week now." I said starting to get pissed.

"For real, why you aint call when you first touched down?" He asked me like he was happy to hear that I was out .

"I had to get some shit straight. What you on, lets meet up and politic. I haven't heard from my right hand in some time now." I purposely put that in there to see what his response would be and just like I thought, the cat got his tongue because he didn't say anything for a minute.

"Man you know how shit get bro but hell yea I can come grab you and we can go to this chicken spot, where you at" He asked me. I gave him the location to the coffee shop by the crib because I didn't want him to know where I was laying my head because I didn't know what our status was at the moment. I thought about getting fully dressed but I decided against it. I kept on what I had on, dabbed a little scented oil on my wrist and threw on my jewelry I had when I came to Sasha's from lock up and walked out the door. Even though she was at work, I shot Sasha a text telling her I was going out to meet up with Nas and I would be back at the house before she got back. The time was about noon and I had to meet up with Bud at midnight, Sasha got off at one in the morning so everything was perfect. I locked the door with the spare key she gave me and stuck it in my wallet and put that in my pocket and proceeded to walk the couple blocks to the coffee shop. I couldn't help but admire the area that Sasha stayed in. Granted, it was a more predominantly white neighborhood but everyone was friendly and that made it that much more easier to tolerate. It took me about five minutes to get to my destination and when I did I sat on their patio and ordered me a water. One thing I was trying to do now that I was a free man was to stay on my healthy shit. I maintained my body this long and I didn't want to get out here and start eating all this good ass food they had. I even told Sasha about cooking all that delicious but unhealthy mess because in the long run it would fuck her system up. I sat and scrolled through all the latest news that was happening in the world while I waited for this nigga to pull up.I thought about reactivating my social media accounts so I can keep up with the latest gossip but I decided against that. My mind was at piece and Facebook and IG would only disturb the inner piece that I was having. I continued to scroll as I heard loud music thumping from some subwoofers that caught my attention. I looked up and saw a clean 2019 Denali turning into the coffee shop parking lot and Nas in the driver seat with a blunt hanging out the corner of his mouth. I couldn't help but shake my head. I grew to learn to act accordingly to your surroundings and when I looked around, all eyes were on Nas and his truck. This was a quiet environment and this nigga wants to come through drawing attention to himself. I stood up and hurriedly walked to the passenger side of Nas car and hopped in and that's when he turned down the new song by DaBaby *Joggers.* Nas peeled out of the parking lot and glanced at me while focusing on the road.

"What the fuck is up my nigga" Nas said as he pounded on my chest lightly with his right hand while keeping his left hand on the steering wheel.

"My manz is free! How are you feeling big homie! I can't call you lil homie no more cuz you sho picked up some weight in that bitch!" Nas said excitedly.

"You know a nigga had to get his weight up. I was tryna be cock diesel in that bitch" I said laughing as I flexed my shoulder muscles. Nas lit the blunt he had dangling in his mouth took a pull from it and handed it to me.

"Na, I'm good ghee. I got a couple more weeks till I'm off papers and I'm blowing back!" I said anticipating the day I can fill my lungs up with the purest Mary Jane I can find.

"Right right" Nas said nodding as he pulled up to Golden Grill cafe in the hood. It was next to a convenience store where multiple niggas hung out slanging weed and work. I sat in deep thought as Nas made a couple plays and sold some green to some of the niggas that were posted.

"You wanna eat in or take the shit to go?" Nas asked.

"You could ride around wit me while I make these moves."

"Yea we could be out, I don't got shit to do until later"

"Cool. I gotta shoot over here South real quick. So what's the news? How long you gone be on papers?" Nas asked me as he ate some of his chicken before getting on the highway.

"Shit I gotta till the end of this month and I aint gone have to deal with these crackas no more." I said as if it was a breath of fresh air.

"You thinking about getting back in?" He asked me and I felt like at the moment was the time to bring up my issues because either we were going to put the shit on the table and leave it or we were going to go our separate ways.

"I might just to get my feet off the ground." I said as I started rubbing my mustache. The car grew silent and I knew he was feeling some type of way.

"So you was just gone let a nigga go down right? You was my nigga Nas and you chose up on me dawg" I said firm but calm. He took a deep breath as to knowing this conversation was bound to happen. Nas rubbed his waves and leaned back in his seat and kept driving, thinking of the right words to say and I let him think while I kept talking.

"Like I aint get not one fucking visit cuz. You stop answering my calls and everything bro! You was my ace, my day one nigga, my brother and I didn't even see you at the trial. You owe me an explanation bro forreal." I told him raising my voice a little. He didn't say anything for a while and shuffled in his seat a bit and shook his head.

"Man I don't know what the fuck I was thinking. You right Los, I coulda held my nigga down and I can admit as a man I was wrong. I let the money take over what was more important and that was loyalty to you my nigga. I know you mad and that's understandable because I would be too." He paused and kept going as we got stuck in highway traffic.

"Meechie told me he was hitting yo books nice for a while and with you being gone, shit the work load doubled up on me nigga so I had to grind that much harder. Iono ghee, I don't know what to say other than I coulda been a better brother."

"Meechie wasn't hitting shit" I told him straight up. I didn't care if he and Meechie was still close I felt like he was full of shit and made Nas turn his back on me and soon after I thought of that, it left my mind. Nas was a grown ass man who could make is own decisions and if he let another man dictate who he fucked with that was some bitch shit.

"I'm sure he wasn't since he in the predicament that you was just in." Nas said as he gave me a disgusting look.

"Fuck that was supposed to mean nigga" I asked him returning the same look he just gave me.

"You snitched Los. How do you think we were supposed to feel"

"Bru I was facing twenty years for some shit that had nothing to do with me but if you accepted a niggas call you would know that now wouldnt you!" I yelled. Nas just drove in silence as we got to his destination and he told his client to come out and get what he needed because we were pulling up. I was not hot and pissed and Nas knew it.

"So let me ask you this. The day I got locked up, when you went back in the house to get Meechie that night did yall know it was a set up? Why you aint come back out? The boys didn't show up until damn near minutes later and I know it aint take that long for you to grab that nigga Meechie and come back out. You knew that nigga was set up or Meechie told you that was a police ass nigga and you never came back out. You couldn't warn me? You let me take the fall for everything that was in that houses bru! Money, work and all them guns in that house and you think I give a fuck about that nigga being locked up when he aint give not one fuck about me!" I was now pissed. This dude had the nerve to pull that shit when he knew what the fuck was going on the whole time.

Nas pulled up to a house and waited for his client to come out to grab the tiny bag of coke that he was about to sell her.

"Yea I knew. When I went in Meechie told me one of the little niggas called him and told him he saw the swat team riding towards the trap and to bounce out the back and that he would grab you from off the porch. He told me yall would meet me at the spot over east so I made my way on foot over there and he showed up without you, I asked where you were at and he told me you got popped off." Nas said as he swerved back into traffic.

"You know what, I aint even bout to stress it dawg it's cool." I said as I shook my head. I really didn't want to talk about the shit no more so I let it go. I rode with Nas for about another hour or so while he finished getting his money and we acted like the previous conversation never happened. After dropping me off back at the spot he met me at I walked back to the crib and started to get ready for my night.

Chapter 18

Sasha

Hitting the snooze button on my phone was my back to reality check as I woke up and prepared for my work day. Normally, I would work the second shift, but I took on a couple morning shift sat the jail to make my checks a little bit bigger. I looked behind me and looked at my fine ass man and couldn't help but smile. Carlos had the juiciest pair of lips that were so full and sweet, and I had to feel them against mine. I turned over to where I was fully facing him and kissed him and gently pulled his bottom lip into my mouth and sucked on it. Los started to stir in his sleep, and I kept kissing him. He struggled to open his eyes but was able to open his left eye and glance at me before closing his eyes again and pulled me closer into him. The smell of Irish Spring invaded my nostrils, and I inhaled deep and loud because Los started laughing at me, and that's when I smelled the horrible odor of morning breath.

"Eww, bae, yo breath on ten," I said as I pulled my face from by his.

"Girl, you wasn't just saying that when you was smelling me, you fucking creep," he said in a low, raspy voice.

"Yeah, you right," I said laughing. I pecked him on the lips as I got out of bed and went to the bathroom to shower and get ready. It had been almost a year since I'd been a corrections officer, and I was satisfied with how things were going. I'd had to deal with the bullshit that came along with the job and the comments from the inmates.

"So, what time you getting off tonight?" he asked me.

"Probably around seven, hopefully earlier," I said as I sat on the edge of the bed and started putting my work pants on.

"Cool," he simply said and closed his eyes and went back to sleep. I finished getting dressed and grabbed my purse from off the door and gave him a kiss goodbye.

"I'm out, boo." I turned the light off and walked out the door.

It had been some time since I'd been clocked in at work, and I had desk duty today. Per usual, I was working with Angie's ghetto ass, and once again, I was left sitting at this desk by myself trying to watch all these damn cameras, but I knew what she was up to. Her boo, Reggie, found a little hideaway spot somewhere in the jail they could get it in at. She told me a while back that he brought her to the spot, but she was too scared to do anything, so they didn't do anything, but over the last couple weeks, she had been disappearing these last couple weeks for too long of a time, and she finally told me what she had been doing. One day while we both coincidentally went on break at the same time, she had showed me the spot. It had been about an hour since she had left for her break, and the supervisor on duty noticed she hadn't clocked back in and came to see if I knew where she was.

"Where's your friend at?" Mathew asked me as he walked up behind me and gave me a stern look.

"I don't know," I said nonchalantly. Whatever she had going on, I didn't want to be a part of, so I stayed out of it.

"Well, when she gets back, tell her to come to my office," Mathew said as he walked away. I waited until I didn't see him anymore and grabbed my phone from out the drawer and texted Angie and told her she needed to get her ass back ASAP. I continued to watch the cameras, and that's when I saw two inmates in each other's face pushing one another.

"Fuck!" I said as I pressed the emergency call light and hopped out of my seat and proceeded to the cell where the inmates were about to go at it. A couple other guards made it to the scene before I did and were already deescalating the situation, and that's when Angie came rushing towards me because she heard the alarm.

"What I miss?" she came up to me and asked.

"A visit from Matthew. He wants to see you in his office," I said as I looked at her and shook her head.

"Damn, for real? You think he noticed I was gone?"

"Hell yeah, he knew you were gone. I ain't 'bout to be getting caught up with your mess, girl. You was gone a whole hour when lunch is only thirty minutes."

"Alright. Since this is handled, I'm gonna go see what he wants," Angie said as she turned around and headed for the stairs. I ignored her and went to fill out the necessary paperwork for the altercation and went back to the desk until my last round. When Angie finally got back to the desk, she had a paper in her hand, and her face looked flushed and red.

"Mmmm. You got yourself written up," I said, laughing at her.

"Hell yeah, his ass wrote me up." Angie laughed like she didn't give not one fuck.

It was time for me to do my last round, so I got up and made my way to the end of the hall to my first cell and did my normal check up until I came across Mac's cell. He was waiting for me at the door, basically blocking my way sight inside so I couldn't see which was a rule breaker when the cells locked down for the night.

"Mac, you know about blocking my view inside. Don't make me open the cell," I told him as I banged on the glass with the butt of my flashlight.

"Where yo mans at?" he asked me with a smirk on his face. I looked around and noticed no other guards were near before answering. I had a feeling Mac knew about me and Los, but he never decided to ask me about it until now.

"I don't know what you talkin' 'bout, inmate, now move out the way," I told him. He stepped to the side so I could look inside but continued to talk.

"You know that nigga gon' get touched with his snitching ass. Rats gotta die," he said to me, and I had a confused look on my face as Mac knew I didn't know what he was talking about.

"Oh, you ain't know? How you think that nigga got out of jail? He a whole rat, and from what I hear, he got money on his head. Better tell that nigga to stay in the house," Mac told me as he turned his back towards me and walked to the toilet and pulled his drawers down to piss. He looked back at me and started laughing, then kissed his finger and touched his ass to basically tell me to kiss his ass. I blew that shit off and kept it moving. I didn't know how to take what he had said. Los told me he got released for good behavior and that some charges got dropped, not for snitching. I was almost off, so I was for sure going to bring it to his attention when I got home. That was on my mind for the rest of my shift which was only about another hour or so, but it went by quick because my mind wasn't focused on the time.

When I finally made it home, I went straight into the kitchen and grabbed my cold bottle of Mango Berry juice and walked in the bedroom and was surprised to see the door was closed. I opened the door and was shocked when I saw Carlos counting this wad of money. I was confused as to where he came up with all that money, so I stood and looked at him until he was done, and he looked up at me and smiled.

"What's up, baby? How was work?" he asked while putting

a rubber band on the money and sticking it in the shoebox he had.

"Um... you tell me, baller," I said while walking to the closest to undress and take my work clothes off and get into something comfortable. He could sense something was wrong, so he put his money up and walked over to the closet where I was.

"What's wrong, mama? Talk to me."

"Um... where did you get that money from?" I asked him. I knew he had money, but this money wasn't adding up. At first, he didn't say anything, and I had to repeat myself because he acted as if he didn't hear me.

"My cousin hit my pockets with some change until I could get on my feet," he answered.

"And you ain't have to do shit for it, he just hit yo pockets, Carlos?" I asked. Once again, he sat there and acted as if he didn't hear me talking to him.

"Los?" I said again, and he cut his eyes at me like he didn't want me to question him. He sat up and looked up at me.

"Alright. I don't want to start lying to you, baby, but I'm not about to tell you exactly what I'm doing in the streets. The less you know, the better. I handled some business for my cousin for a couple bucks."

"Handled some business?" I asked him.

"Yes. It's not what you think, boo, I promise, but I'm not saying it won't get there. I can't just sit around waiting on no bullshit as job to pay me less than I'm worth," Carlos said to me and waited for me to respond. That wasn't what was heavy on my mind at the moment, so I didn't say anything else about it.

"So, when I was doing my rounds today, Mac brought something up to my attention," I said as I sat on the bed facing him.

"What he say?" Los asked me, looking wide-eyed.

"He said you snitched and that's how you got released," I said flat out. Wasn't no point of trying to beat around the bush. Since Los hadn't responded, I continued.

"He also said to watch yo back because some niggas is at you. Look Los, I want to be with you, but I don't want to be looking over my shoulder everyday over some bullshit that has nothing to do with me," I said as I looked at him with concern in my eyes. For a second, it looked like he was now in deep thought about what I said, and for some reason, I thought what Mac said was true.

"It's true, huh?" Your silence is telling me that it's true. You told on someone, and now he sending people at you, Carlos?" I asked him, and yet he was still ignoring me, so I walked in front of him and lifted his head with my hand so he could look me in my face.

"We just started this relationship, and I'd rather not continue with a lie. Tell me wassup so I won't have no surprises, Los!" I said, getting loud. He turned me around so I would be sitting on his lap and laid his head on my back as he wrapped his hands around my waist.

"I'm not proud of what I did, Sasha. Yeah, I snitched on the nigga. The only reason I'm telling you this because I don't want you to be left in the dark if some shit hit the fan, so yes, I snitched, Sash. I was facing twenty fucking years for some shit that I had nothing to do with, ma. The niggas that I thought was my main manz switched up on me. Meechie didn't even show no support at all, and I was doing the time for that nigga. So yeah, I told on his ass, and to the streets, that may lessen my street cred and manhood, but fuck that and fuck them. I ain't livin' for none of them niggas but me cuz clearly, when the shit hit the fan, they said fuck me and let me take the fall for all that shit, and most of the shit they was throwing at me I have never heard of, but do you think they cared? Fuck no. All the cops knew was that they had someone they can pin the charges on and close the case so they can move on and fuck up someone else's life," Los said, shaking his head. I got up and sat beside him so he could have my full attention.

"Now them niggas mad because the charges that I was facing, is what Meechie is now facing, and they don't like that shit. See, when it was me, niggas didn't give a fuck, but now, they big homie down and out, muthafuckas wanna point the finger. Well, fuck 'em!" Los picked up the money he was counting when I walked in and threw it back on the bed.

"This shit ain't shit. Yeah, I got my feet wet a little and delivered some work. I'm not about to be sitting in this house all fucking day not doing shit. Sasha, I'm a felon, they was trying to charge me for murder; now you tell me what kind of job I was gone' get? What job could I have held down that would allow me to provide for you the right way, Mookie?" he asked me, calling me by my nickname. At that point ,I didn't know what to say to him. He had every right to do what he had to do, and I didn't blame him not one bit. I scooted closer to him and grabbed his head and laid it on my shoulders. My baby was hurting, and I could see it all in his face. I didn't want to make matters worse, so I left it alone and was about to start cleaning the bed off so we could lay down and relax.

"Na, boo. I'ma go have me a drink," he said as he looked at me.

"You sure you should be going anywhere after what I just told you?" I asked him.

"If they gon' get me, they gon' do it. I'm not about to let no nigga that bleed like me stop me from enjoying life. It's a little hole in the wall I saw when I stepped out with Nas earlier that looked lowkey and cool. I'ma meet one of the homies, and I'ma be back. It's early, momma, and I don't plan on staying out too late."

Los threw the money at me and got up to get dressed.

"Count that up for me and put it up in a safe place, and tomorrow, we gotta talk, boo. I'm thinking about getting back in the drug game, and if you gon' be with me, I need to know that, and if you don't, I need to know that too. As you can see, shit ain't all peaches with me right now, and you're right. I don't want you having to look over your shoulder for my bullshit, so I'ma let you think about it, and have that pussy ready for me when I get back," Los said as he bent down and gave me a kiss as his phone started to ring. He answered, and I heard a male voice telling him he was about to be at the spot to pick him up.

"Bud 'bout to be on his way. I got him meeting me at the coffee shop. Don't wait up, baby, nor do I want you to worry. I'ma be alright," Los said as he stood in the doorway and waited for me to say something.

"OK, Carlos," was all I was able to give him. I had a lot to think about, so maybe it was good that he was leaving for a couple hours. I gave him a kiss before he walked out the door and walked back in my room and counted the money like he asked me to do. Five grand in the mixture of tens, twenties, and hundreds was in the knot I counted, and I put it up in the closet inside a pair of brand new heels that still had the tag on it and that were still in the box. I straightened up the house a bit before taking me a nice, hot shower and chilling for the night. I had a lot to think about, and I knew Carlos was about to give me a run for my money, and honestly, I was ready for whatever.

Chapter 19

Los

After finally calming Sasha's nerves, I headed out to meet Bud at the coffee shop. He told me one of his other boys were supposed to be meeting us at the bar called Willard's in the hood. We used to always be in the bar taking shot after shot just chilling so I was aware of the crowd that might be in there tonight. I told her we were going to a lowkey bar because I didn't want her to worry about all the hood niggas and gold-digging females at Willard's. We pulled up along the side of the bar behind the other slew of cars and parked and chopped it up for a minute before getting out. Bud knew of the situation I was in and knew about me ratting on dude, but being that was my blood cousin, he ain't treat me no different but stayed keeping it real with me.

"Look in the glove compartment," he said as he smoked his blunt. The way that weed was smelling made me want to hit the blunt, but I knew I had to stay clean for another two weeks before I was off papers, and I couldn't wait! I wanted to smoke with Sasha, but of course, she kept a nigga on his toes, so she wouldn't even smoke around me. I opened the compartment and there was a Smith and Wesson sitting on top of the papers he had in there.

"That's yours, baby. All clean, no prints or bodies, cousin," he said as I took it out and examined the gun. It was like as soon as I picked the gun up, the hood Los came to surface and was ready to get back in business and earn a name for myself again. Doing those two years behind bars would have a nigga wanting to get on the straight path, but once you got out and saw it wasn't as easy as you thought it would be to get back on your feet, it would make you get back to your original self. I tucked the gun in my waist band and we got out of the car. I wasn't worried about getting searched at the door because Ducey, the boucer was one of my niggas from back in the day before I got locked up so I knew he was cool.

"Los baby, what's good, my nigga?" Ducey said as I walked in the entrance after Bud. I slapped five with Ducey and chopped it up with him for a hot second before proceeding in the jam-packed bar. It was like a party just for me tonight because everyone I knew was in this bitch, so I knew it was definitely gonna be a vibe. Bud and I walked up to the bar, and he ordered our first couple drinks, and we got a table that wasn't too close to the DJ so we could chop it up. He handed me a henny and coke, and I sipped on that while I looked around the not so big bar.

"So, what you think about the drop?" he asked me while looking at this light-skinned shorty that was throwing that ass all around the mini dance floor.

"Shit, it was easy money. Too easy for me, cousin. You know how I get down!" I said loudly over the music.

"Yeah, but you know we gotta make sure you still know how to throw the ball before we make you the pitcher," Bud said. Everybody was live and turning up as some old school Nate Dogg blasted through the speakers. It had been about an hour since we first got in the bar, and it was now packed to capacity. Bud stood up and looked towards the doorway, and I followed his eyes and saw a dude walking up towards us, and I assumed it was the dude he said was meeting us there. The two men dapped up, and Bud gestured for me so stand up so I could meet his friend.

"Los, this my nigga, Fab. Fab, this my cousin, Los, the one I was tellin' y'all about at Ant crib," Bud said to Fab.

"What's good, my dude?" I said to him as we slapped hands

and sat back down at the table.

"I don't remember it being this muthafuckin' lit in this bitch before," I said as I started to feel the effects of the drinks I was throwing back. The night was seeming like it was never going to end as I actually sat and enjoyed myself. I noticed it was this dark-skinned beauty that kept eyeing me from the bar, and by the way her and her homegirls kept looking our way, I knew she was going to come over and shoot her shot, and I was correct. It was three of them total and three of us, so I knew what they were on already, and I wanted no part in any of it, but I played along anyway.

"Hey, wassup? I'm Mimi," she said, holding her hand out for mine. I had to admit that shorty was fine as fuck, and if I wasn't with Sasha, I probably would have entertained her more than I was.

"I'm Los," I said nonchalantly as I shook her hand. She took that as a Cue to sit next to me, and her friends started entertaining Bud and Fab that were clearly going.

"Nice to meet you. Have I seen you somewhere before?" Mimi asked me, pondering on her own thoughts.

"I don't think so, mami," I said as I kept drinking my now forth drink and looking around at my surroundings.

"Well, can I get to know you?" She asked me as she stood up and walked between my legs and inserted herself on my lap. I was shocked and looked over at Bud who was laughing his ass off. I politely pushed her off of me, and she tried to sit back down in my lap. Oh, this bitch was bold. I pushed her off of me again, but this time with a little more force. She stumbled a little bit and turned and looked at me like I had two heads or something.

"Damn, was it that serious, nigga?" She asked me as she twisted her face at me.

"Yeah, did I invite your ass on my lap? No, I did not," I said as I sat back in my chair and smiled at the now pissed off Mimi. Her homegirl said something to her that I couldn't hear due to the music blasting. She waved her hand at me dismissive like and walked off with her girls. Bud and Fab were looking at me like I was crazy, and we all busted out laughing. It was too many diseases going around for me to want to fuck on a random female when I had my own pussy waiting on me at the crib. We kicked it and vibed the whole night until some niggas started arguing and looking like they were about to be on bullshit, so we decided to head out to Denny's restaurant. Fab got dropped off at the bar, so he hopped in the car with us. Bud and Fab both started rolling a couple blunts, and somehow, these niggas had a bottle of Hennessey in the car. I didn't know how it got in there because I didn't see it when I first got in the car nor did I see Fab with it before he got in. We weren't that far from the restaurant, so Bud blasted his music as we rode through the hood to our destination. It was about one in the morning, and it was a Friday night, so the police were out heavy tonight, and I was the only one that noticed it.

As we got to the last stop light before we had to turn into the parking lot, a squad car pulled behind us. They had just put the blunt out, and all the windows were rolled down, so I knew the cops smelled the Mary Jane through their windows. Just when the light turned green for us to turn, the police started flashing their lights for us to stop.

"Fuck!" I said to no one in particular. This was exactly what I didn't need at the moment. I was a freshly released felon, and I couldn't be around drugs or guns, and that was exactly what was in the car with me. I smoothly grabbed the gun that I had concealed in my pants and stuck it back in the back of the passenger seat before the boys got out their squad car. I started to hyperventilate a little as my anxiety was starting to get the best of me. I contemplated on making a run for it, but that would have just made things worse than they could be, so I decided to stay put. One officer walked up to the driver's window and flashed his flashlight all throughout the car. He asked Bud for his license and registration, and that's when I saw another cop walking to the passenger side window. I was glad I decided to sit in the back this time because it seemed like these cops were on straight bullshit. The other cop asked Fab for his credentials, and that's when the drama started. Fab was refusing to answer any of the officer's questions and making this situation more difficult than it actually needed to be.

"Sir, all I asked of you was to give me your name," the white cop said as he shined the light from Fab back to me.

"Man, fuck that. You ain't have no reason to stop us in the first place. All we wanted to do was get some food and head back to the crib, but y'all bored asses wanted to fuck with us," an intoxicated Fab said to the officers.

"If I were you, I would watch your mouth," the officer that was on the driver side said.

"Yo, chill nigga, 'for you get us popped off," Bud said to Fab with an aggravated look on his face.

"Roll your window down, son," the cop said to me. Shit, once they ran my name, I knew it would pop up that I just got out, and it was mandatory that they contacted my P.O to let him know I came in contact with the police.

"What's your name and birthday?" he asked me. Something told me I should lie, and that's what I did.

"Monte Steph-" I started to say but was cut off when the police got a call on their radio yelling code ten-thirty-one, which meant a crime in progress.

"Today must be your lucky day, boys," the officer said as they all ran back to their squad cars and drove off, leaving us in silence as we sat there.

"Y'all niggas was scared shitless!" I said as I busted out laughing, and Bud peeled off back into the street.

"Nah, you was scared, nigga. Who the fuck is Monte?" Bud asked me as he glanced at me through the rearview mirror.

"Shit, iono, but he wasn't about to get my real name. I ain't tryna go back to jail no time soon, nigga," I said laughing.

"Aye, I ain't even hungry no more, dawg," Fab said, drunk and slurring his words

"After that, me either, honestly. I just wanna go lay under my bitch," I said as I laid my head on the back seat. It seemed like the liquor always hit harder on the drive home from the club.

"Ight, I'm bout to drop y'all drunk niggas off and go home, fuck it," Bud said. I closed my eyes for what seemed like a second and ended up being almost thirty minutes late. I woke up to Bud calling my name telling me he was at the coffee shop where he picked me up. I was drunk and didn't feel like walking the rest of the way back to the crib, so I just gave him the directions to my exact destination. When we pulled to the front of our duplex, I sat and talked with Bud before going in.

"Yo man is crazy, cuz. Dude almost got all us whacked talking to the boys like that," I said to Bud. The boys was what we called the police in Minnesota.

"Man, I know, buddy was ripping, but he cool as hell though. His boy Ant is who I get green from, so you will be seeing and working a lot with Fab, so you might as well get used to it. By the way, he said it's cool that I bring you by his crib so y'all can meet and discuss business," Bud said as he took the blunt out the ashtray and lit it.

"He knows about my case?" I asked him.

"He knows you were locked up, and that's all he needs to know right now. Look, cuz, what you did was wrong in the eye of the streets, but oh well, what's done is done. Don't keep trip ping about that shit. Either you gon' chalk that shit up and keep making your bread, or you gon let the street get the best of you, and that will be your downfall," Bud said to me, and that was some real shit.

"Na, I'ma get this money and say fuck them other niggas."

"Bet, then let's get to it. I'ma come grab you sometime tomorrow after I talk to that nigga and see when a good time would be to come through, and you just be ready."

"Bet," I said as I slid out of the car and grabbed my Smith and Wesson out the back seat. I walked up to the door and put my key in the lock. I turned around to see Bud pulling out the parking lot, and I noticed another car sitting there with the engine running, but the lights weren't on. I didn't see anybody in the driver's seat, so I brushed it off and stumbled in the house.

The smell of lavender candles hit my nostrils, and I looked around to see the place was lit with candles that decorated the tables.

"Bae!" I called out to Sasha as I walked to the kitchen and grabbed a banana off the counter. I needed something to soak up the liquor that was now swirling around in my stomach.

I walked back into the living room and started taking off my shoes because I knew how she felt about shoes in the house.

"Sash-" I was turned around starting to yell her name but stopped when I saw her standing in the bedroom doorway with a sexy black negligee and some heels. I was in awe as she sashayed her way towards me.

"Damn, Mookie," I said as she walked up on me, pressing her breastS to my chest. The smell of dove body wash and some sort of seducing perfume danced in my nose.

"How was your night?" Sasha asked me as she stood on her tippy toes and started kissing my neck and kissing me all over my face.

"It was good. I'm a little intoxicated, mami," I said as she pulled me to the couch. I turned my head to make sure the curtains were closed on the windows and let her take over.

"I know you are. I'm ready for that henny dick. Can I take advantage of you, baby?" she asked me as she stood up and took a couple steps backwards. She grabbed her phone off the table and turned the Bluetooth speaker on and let Daniel Caesar *Best Part* play. Sasha started to wind her hips to the beat as she let her hands caress herself.

Damn, she is fucking gorgeous, I said to myself. I felt my blood rush to the right part of my body, and I had to undo my shorts because the bulge needed to be let loose. I released my dick from my boxers without leaving her eye contact and stroked my now rock-solid dick.

It was now standing at attention, and I put both of my hands on the back of the couch, with my shorts and boxers around my ankles as I watched my beautiful goddess shake and twist that fat ass. She slowly walked towards me and kicked her heels to the side and got on her knees. She was about to bless me with the greatest head I had and would ever receive. I was still feeling my liquor, so when I leaned my head back and closed my eyes, the room started spinning a little bit. The warm feeling of Sasha's mouth covering the head of my dick brought me back to life. I looked down at her and she was staring at me while making circular motions over the head of my dick with her tongue, and that shit was driving me wild.

I grunted under my breath and started moving my hips a little because she was either giving me that sloppy toppy or the alcohol was just doing its job. Sasha was now deep throating the dick and had me moaning like a little bitch.

"Fuck, baby, keep doin' that shit," I moaned as I was damn near fucking her mouth. I couldn't take it anymore, so I stood up and switched places with her. I pushed her down on the couch and spread her legs. I slid her panties to the side and started eating the meal that I didn't get to make it to while I was out. Her pussy smelled of Dove soap, and it was freshly waxed, so my face glided over them lips nicely. I sucked on her clit while I made a 'come here' motion with my finger in her insides. Sasha arched her back and thrust her hips forward. I spread her pussy lips with my fingers, acting as a peace sign and went to work. I stuck my tongue in her pussy and shook my head side to side as I reached up and fondled with her titties that were now out of her negligee.

"Oh, my goodness. Los, baby, shit," Sasha moaned as she couldn't stay still. I could tell she was on the verge of ecstasy when glass started shattering everywhere.

POP! POP! POP! POP! POP!

Bullets started flying through the front door and the window at lightning speed.

"Get down!" I yelled at Sasha as I pulled her off the couch by her feet so she was firmly on the floor.

"Carlos!" she screamed at the top of her lungs as I raced to the chest that I threw the gun on when I walked in the house. I pulled my boxers up just as Sasha was trying to make her way to me even with bullets flying everywhere.

POP! POP! POP!

The shots kept coming through the window. I took the clip out to make sure there were bullets in it, and luckily, there was. I looked through the peephole and saw a black car with one single shooter aiming at the living room. I flung the door open and started banging the hammer. The car sped off, and I ran into the parking lot still shooting until my clip was empty. I looked around the streets and noticed they were still empty, and I ran back into the house. Our duplex was now riddled with bullet holes, and I knew it had something to do with me instantly. I ran into the house to find Sasha lying in the corner bleeding.

"Fuck, baby! Where you shot at?" I asked. Sasha was screaming hysterically as I was moving her around to see where she had been hit. Luckily, she was shot in the shoulder, and it went straight through, so I knew she would be good.

"Baby, I'm sorry," I kept saying to her as I heard the sirens get louder. I was trying to get her as comfortable as possible before the police started swarming the house. I couldn't stay here. I had to bounce before the boys got there because I was determined not to go back to jail.

"Baby, it hurts," Sasha cried to me.

I stood up and paced the floor walking over all the shattered glass. I had to think about what the fuck I was going to do. I know Sasha was going to be pissed with me but I had to think quick.

"Baby, I gotta go!" I said as I grabbed my shorts off the floor and shook the glass off them and started putting them on. The bullets flying through the windows helped sober me up with a quickness.

"No Los please don't leave baby what am I gonna do" Sasha asked me trying to get up.

"Don't move baby. I can't go back to jail baby I just cant" I said now in tears. I did not want to leave her but I knew I had to or I wouldn't see the light of day again.

"I will be back tomorrow, baby. You know what it is, love. Please, baby, you know to keep me out of it. I promise you I am not leaving you, but I gotta go before they get here. Call Bud as soon as you get out the hospital, baby," I said, kissing her repeatedly. The police were right around the corner because the sirens got louder, and I couldn't stay any longer. I scribbled Bud's number down on the paper she kept in the living room and kissed her one last time before I disappeared into the night.

"I'ma be back, mami. I love you, baby!"

Fuck! Now I gotta let the street nigga Los resurface cuz these niggas got me all the way fucked up!

TO BE CONTINUED…..

WANT TO INTERACT WITH T'ANN MARIE & HER TEAM? JOIN OUR READERS GROUP ON FACEBOOK @ *T'ANN MARIE PRESENTS: THE HOUSE OF URBAN LITERACY*! WIN PRIZES, BE APART OF LIVE BOOK DISCUSSIONS & MORE!

Are you looking for a publishing home that will mold you to become a better writer?

T'Ann Marie Presents, is now accepting submissions in the following genres:

*Urban Fiction
*Romance
*Street Lit
*Paranormal
*BWWM
*Erotica
*Women's Fiction
*Christian Fiction

For consideration, please submit the first 3 chapters of your finished manuscript & contact information to:

TAnnMarieSubs@gmail.com

Let us make your dreams, Reality!

Want to join our mailing list?!

Just send your email address by text to:

Text

TMPUPNEXT

to 22828 to get started.

Message and data rates may apply.

CPSIA information can be obtained
at www.ICGtesting.com
Printed in the USA
LVHW051628251119
638450LV00006B/1106/P